S0-AAB-063

Fire licked the ancient church with the hot tongue of death

Keio and Rafael stormed through the sacred structure turned hellground.

They worked together like a micro-army. Their mission: save McCarter.

Time perished. The fire ate more and more of the building. In the basement, bound at the wrists and ankles, McCarter watched the man-eating flames lunge closer.

He had no intention of dying. But it looked as if he had no other choice....

"Some of the largest friends you could have. The Bolan team is clearly the best in the business."
—*Navy News*

Mack Bolan's
PHOENIX FORCE

Mack Bolan's
ABLE TEAM

MACK BOLAN
The Executioner

PHOENIX FORCE

AN EXECUTIONER SERIES

The Fury Bombs

Gar Wilson

A GOLD EAGLE BOOK FROM

W🌐RLDWIDE

TORONTO · NEW YORK · LONDON

The cover is a detail of a larger painting entitled *Campaign Portrait*, commissioned by Mack Bolan, which hangs at Stony Man Farm.

First edition May 1983

Special thanks and acknowledgment to Robert Hoskins for his contribution to this work.

ISBN 0-373-61305-9

Copyright © 1983 by Worldwide Library.
Philippine copyright 1983. Australian copyright 1983.

All rights reserved. Except for use in any review, the reproduction or utilization of this work in whole or in part in any form by any electronic, mechanical or other means, now known or hereafter invented, including xerography, photocopying and recording, or in any information storage or retrieval system, is forbidden without the permission of the publisher, Worldwide Library, 225 Duncan Mill Road, Don Mills, Ontario, Canada M3B 3K9. All the characters in this book have no existence outside the imagination of the author and have no relation whatsoever to anyone bearing the same name or names. They are not even distantly inspired by any individual known or unknown to the author, and all the incidents are pure invention.

The Gold Eagle trademark, consisting of the words GOLD EAGLE and the portrayal of an eagle, and the Worldwide trademark, consisting of the word WORLDWIDE in which the letter "O" is represented by a depiction of a globe, are trademarks of Worldwide Library.

Printed in Canada

1

FIVE GOOD MEN against a world infested with terror goons.

Five men moving through a world of nightmares where treachery lurks behind every door—a world where bright sunshine casts shadows that conceal cutthroats and assassins; a world where smiles hide hatreds that fester; a world in which men strike out at the innocent and the trusting, at young and old, at all who abide the law.

Some call it patriotism, but it is a madman's patriotism that destroys rather than preserves, that uses gun, sword and bomb to murder children in their schools, worshipers in their churches, bystanders in crowded streets.

The bombs explode and the submachine guns spray steel- and copper-jacketed death, tearing bodies and rending limbs until those who survive count lucky those who died.

Some call it patriotism; some believe it moral as they act in the name of blood-thirsty religions and blood-thirsty gods. Some know only greed as reason for sabotage and murder and war. Call it what they will, there is only one true name for the hellish deeds, the terrible crimes committed, the mad lust for blood, power and money that threaten to destroy all.

Terrorism.

Five good men against terrorism.

Five men against a world watched by the gods of evil who huddle in the darkest corners of hell, plotting The End.

Five men—the *best* of the *best*.

They are Phoenix Force.

GARY MANNING WAS AWAKE and working early. He walked through the corridors of his Montreal offices, stopping occasionally to check unfinished paperwork on desks, and to scan a report that recommended upgrading security at an electronics plant in suburban Louisville, Kentucky. Gary's business was security consulting that extended to supplying guards and installing sophisticated alarm systems to the private sector and to the governments of Canada and the United States.

That was Gary Manning's business....

Phoenix Force was his life.

He prowled restlessly, unable to light, to settle. Once he paused, held aside a curtain and looked out at the view across Dominion Square and Place du Canada. A moment, at his desk, later he tried to concentrate on a design for a new alarm system. Three minutes later he threw it aside in frustration. He rose in a quick, lithe movement to resume prowling the corridors.

They were out there somewhere, the vermin, planning murder, plotting revolution. They were everyplace where men knew a measure of freedom. They subcribed to different political faiths, but behind the slogans and the false patriotism they were all the same.

The pager clipped to Manning's belt began to beep, the demanding tone repeating twice each second.

He stopped pacing, the impatient scowl on his face smoothing, the lines of worry that furrowed his forehead disappearing. He hit the button to kill the clamor, and in the same instant headed for his office where two telephones sat on his desk. He grabbed the red instrument, a phone with a scrambler device, and lifted the receiver.

"Manning."

The connection—a direct open line that was maintained between Manning's offices in several major cities in which he did business and Stony Man Farm, the largest and most efficient antiterrorist base in the world—clicked in.

He listened to the voice on the other end of the line then said, "I'm on my way, Stony Man." Quickly he replaced the instrument and headed toward the door. The bastards were trying to set the world on fire again.

OF THE FIVE PHOENIX FORCE AGENTS, only Manning was awake at that hour of the morning. Keio Ohara was in his apartment in Alameda,

California, enjoying a brief vacation before returning to his home in Tokyo. He woke instantly at the summons of the beeper, then rose from his sleeping mat with the red telephone in hand.

"Ohara," he said, then he listened.

Plans were immediately forgotten.

As Keio listened, his heartbeat sped from the slow pace of sleep until, within thirty seconds of awakening, he was at the peak of alertness, ready for action.

"I understand," Keio said. "I'll stand by for further orders."

He replaced the receiver and stood holding the telephone a moment longer. He then set it on the floor, in its usual position next to the sleeping mat, and walked out onto the balcony.

It was a few hours before dawn. Cool breezes swept off San Francisco Bay. The street below was deserted. It was quiet, deceptively quiet.

Out in the night, innocent men were dead.

YAKOV KATZENELENBOGEN, formerly of Mossad, the Israeli secret service, stirred in his sleep and tried to brush away an annoying insect. The bug continued its insistent chirping.

"Yakov!" A hand grabbed his shoulder and shook him. "Wake up. It's your pager."

Jerusha Steckler shook him again. Yakov blinked, raised an arm and stared at his watch. Gray dawn filtered into the New York City apartment overlooking Sutton Place and the

East River. It was close to seven. Jerusha rose from the bed and padded into the kitchen. He could hear her rattling dishes as he sat up and reached for the telephone on the nightstand.

This was not a secure instrument. Katz was not in one of the places he maintained as a secure base between assignments, but the summons could not be ignored. He punched out a number and waited as it rang three times. The phone was answered by the same duty man who had spoken to Gary and Keio.

"Katz," said the commander of Phoenix Force. Katz then took in the information.

"Have a car downstairs in fifteen minutes," Katz ordered when the voice at the other end stopped.

He hung up without waiting for an acknowledgment, stood and began looking for his clothes. The strong smell of coffee filled the apartment by the time he finished dressing. Jerusha met him at the bedroom door with a cup.

"You'll be back?" she asked.

"Of course."

"I won't ask when."

"Thank you . . . I'll miss you."

She smiled as he drained the cup. She took it back, proffered her cheek for a perfunctory kiss, then followed him to the door. When the door closed behind him, she sighed and returned to the kitchen with the cup. She knew he would return.

WITH NO FURTHER ACTION IN SIGHT after Phoenix Force had decimated the terrorists who had tried to spill the blood of millions to avenge the horror of Hiroshima, Rafael Encizo, like Gary Manning, had seized the opportunity and time to return to his business, marine insurance investigating. Unlike Gary, Rafael was able to concentrate on his work. He was in Houston, his first stop before reporting to Galveston where he was to investigate a suspicious and possibly spurious claim against one of the insurance companies that kept him on retainer.

Rafael's business was small, but successful. Not a bad step forward for a man who, after being captured in the Bay of Pigs invasion, had been a prisoner of Castro.

Like Yakov, Rafael was not alone when his beeper sounded. A querulous voice emerged from the pillow beside him. He slapped his companion on her ample rump, bringing a sharp curse, then he dressed quickly and left the unsecured hotel room.

It took nearly ten minutes before he reached the phone he wanted, in a booth on a street corner. Rafael kicked the door shut and placed the call to Stony Man.

The message was brief, the orders the same as those given to Keio.

"All right," Rafael replied, "I might as well take care of the business that brought me here while I wait. I'll be moving around some, but I'm ready to break off at any time."

A broad smile passed across Rafael's face. He made a fist with his right hand and rubbed it with his left.

Action. Another chance to hit back. Another chance to even the score against the scum of the world.

Rafael laughed and for a moment he forgot the woman waiting in his hotel room. Like Gary, he had suddenly been handed a breath of new life.

IN LONDON, David McCarter—although it was midday and despite the hum of traffic on Kensington Road outside—came out of a deep and dreamless sleep of utter exhaustion, knowing that someone had entered his room—someone who moved in darkness, moved with a hatred so overpowering it threatened sanity, a hatred that would be satisfied only with death. . . .

2

THE GIANT C-130 AIR FORCE CARGO PLANE made a lazy circle over Mohawk Valley, one raised wing tip shredding the bottom of a leaden cloud. The pilot made an adjustment to the controls, a pulse beating visibly in his throat. His skin crawled, shrinking from contact with the muzzle of the Kalashnikov AK-47 assault rifle that was held six inches from his neck by a man wearing a stolen Air Force uniform.

"You're doin' wonderful, Major," the gunman told the pilot.

The gunman was one of two Irish terrorists in the cockpit of the hijacked plane.

The terrorist in the copilot's seat smiled, and Major Joseph Collins, USAF, commander of the C-130, swallowed hard. The major's complexion was sickly beneath his tan. The middle finger of his left hand tapped a nervous beat against the yoke, while his eyes flicked across the instrument panel, unseeing. His thoughts raced in turmoil.

Throw the ship into a power dive, Collins thought. *That'll knock the bastard gunman off his feet and give Jessup a chance to take the other son of a bitch! Do it! Do it now!*

But Collins did nothing to the plane.

He felt the butterfly patch over one eyebrow that covered a deep cut. He also felt sore ribs and a beaten cheekbone, the pains of his first attempt to fight these bastards. Fighting would not work.

He shuddered, remembering how they had stormed into his house that morning and had taken his wife, Jill, and his three children hostage. Collins swallowed again, his throat constricted, raw.

The terrorist with the Kalashnikov shifted his weight. "How long are we going to be flyin' around in circles?"

"Patience," said the other hardguy. "The major will have us down as soon as he can."

The terrorists all seemed to be Irish, the two in the cockpit, who were obviously in charge, and the others who had taken the places of the regular crew.

The man with the Kalashnikov wore fatigues with master sergeant's stripes, the shirt tight around his chest. The stenciled name over his breast pocket read T.T. Eckstrom.

The real T.T. Eckstrom was dead. He had died earlier that day trying to keep the shirt on his back.

"We'll take your shirt, Sergeant," the leader of the terrorists had said.

Eckstrom had scowled and replied, "You'll take nothing, you son of a bitch."

The Irishman sighed. "A stubborn man. Do as you must."

"Sergeant, don't argue!" warned Collins. "Do as he says!"

But the warning had come too late. A rifle butt smashed the back of Eckstrom's skull and he sagged to his knees. As Eckstrom fought to keep conscious, two of the terrorists had grabbed him by the arms and stripped him of the shirt.

They'd given the shirt to the man who wore it now. When he'd finished buttoning it, sucking in his gut to allow the buttons to go through the buttonholes, he'd pulled the service .45 he wore in a regulation holster and worked the slide. He placed the muzzle three inches from the bridge of Eckstrom's nose.

"Not that way!" said the leader. "Do it with feeling."

The crew of the C-130 were good friends. Most of them were young; several, little more than teenagers. They all watched in horror as the man who wore Eckstrom's shirt methodically kicked the sergeant to death. One fainted, another puked.

Joe Collins was made painfully aware of what would happen to his family if he did not do exactly as these men said.

The bogus Eckstrom shifted again, eyes darting occasionally to the navigator, First Lieutenant Ronald Jessup. Jessup was little more than a youth himself. He and Collins were the only members of the original crew still aboard.

The radio crackled as voices spoke to aircraft flying the skies of central and northern New York. Collins ignored the voices and adhered to the holding pattern the plane had been in for the past twenty minutes. His eyes automatically checked fuel consumption. There was plenty left in the tanks. He made a trim adjustment, not even thinking about it, his hands reaching instinctively.

Terrorists or no terrorists, he could not let this plane and its cargo fall from the sky. The cargo bay held a dozen twenty-one-foot rubber-tired trailers, in three rows of four. Canvas-shrouded, they were tied down with cables, the wheels chocked to prevent shifting. Each shroud carried the yellow trefoil of a nuclear warning.

Joe Collins knew the terrorists had taken and stashed four nuclear warheads—replacing them with fakes—but he also knew that the warheads left on the plane had enough power to blast a very large crater between the cities of Utica and Rome. Collins remembered what the scientists had told him—that the warheads would probably remain secure if the plane crashed. But....

The Irishman in the copilot's seat looked at the chronometer on the panel and checked it against his watch, as though he did not trust the Air Force's procurement system. He wore the stolen name tag and captain's bars of the man who should have been Collins's copilot on this flight, an Air Force careerist named Hamilton Brownlow.

The real Brownlow was almost two thousand miles away, murdered in the cellar of Collins's house.

Like Eckstrom, Ham Brownlow had become a casualty in the terrorist war.

Half an hour after the terrorists had taken over the Collinses' house, a two-acre ranchette on a back road, Ham Brownlow had arrived, eager to renew an old friendship. He and Collins had served and flown together, but Ham had been stationed in Amarillo the past two years. This would be their first flight together since Ham's transfer.

When Ham arrived, the terrorists' van was in the closed garage. The Collinses' car waited in the driveway, innocently. He never suspected a thing.

Brownlow's neck was snapped in two by a terrorist the second he entered the door.

Brownlow was dead.

Eckstrom was dead.

Do as they say, Collins thought, or they would all be dead.

Collins shuddered again. Sweat trickled coldly down his back. He could smell his own fear.

Please God, he prayed, *let me wake from this nightmare and find the world sane again.*

The lives of the eight remaining crew members depended on Collins. Also, the lives of his wife and his three kids depended entirely on his obeying these Irish terrorists.

Collins glanced at Jessup. The young man smiled weakly. The sleeve of Jessup's flight suit was stained dark with blood. He had cradled the dead body of his friend Eckstrom, trying to will the man to breathe again.

A mile below, Utica and Rome and their satellite villages wheeled in a majestic turning as the plane circled, the residents blissfully ignorant of the deadly cargo overhead. The valley was grimy after spring rains had turned the ground to mud. There were vestiges of winter snow in the higher elevations, but the marshes between the twin tracks of the Barge Canal and the Mohawk River were as gray as the sky.

The flight path carried the C-130 into the clouds for a moment and Collins switched on the wipers. The rubber blades beat a harsh tempo. He stole a glance at the Irishman, his eyes drawn by the face of the devil.

The sea-ruddied face under a cap of black curls seemed almost boyish, but there were lines of age around the cold, piercing blue eyes. And then, aware of Collins's study, he smiled, revealing a crooked incisor.

Collins looked away from the bastard.

His thoughts drifted back to the terrorists'

invasion of his home. The scum had shoved his wife downstairs by slamming a foot into the small of her back. His son, Bobby, had let out one terrible roar and had gone for the terrorist before his father could intervene. The boy had dived into a smashing pistol butt that sent him to the floor, his cheek laid open.

Collins had gone crazy. It had taken three terrorists to drag him down, one on each arm and another sitting on his legs.

"Don't kill him," ordered the leader. "We need the major alive. Just teach him a small lesson."

That was when Collins had got the marks. His body ached. He had a hundred pains but the worst was the look on the faces of his kids as they watched their father being ruthlessly stomped.

"Enough?" the Irishman had asked.

Collins sucked in air, gasped, "Enough!"

"That was a foolish thing to do, Major." The smile had vanished. "You have two attractive daughters. The men I'm leaving with them have rape on their charge sheets, although they'll hang for more serious crimes if they're ever taken by the Brits. Think of your daughters, Major."

Collins had seen the gleam of anticipation in the eyes of one of the hoodlums left to guard his family. The memory sickened him. Animals!

Collins would do what the terrorists said,

everything they said, to hold onto the slim hope that his family might be spared.

The radio crackled: this time the message was for the C-130. Collins and Jessup tensed at their call letters.

"Acknowledge, Major," ordered the Irishman.

Collins obeyed and was given landing instructions. He took the plane from its holding pattern into the approach, and five minutes later they were on the ground.

The C-130 rolled onto an empty hardstand, two yellow foam-pumper fire trucks and an ambulance moving parallel to their track. The plane stopped. The fire trucks and ambulance veered off and returned to station. A gasoline tanker, and a blue tractor used to tow airplanes away from the loading gates, waited at the hardstand.

Collins killed the engines and the vibration stopped. He removed his headphones and got up, moving stiffly after hours in the pilot's seat. He walked back through the belly of the plane, followed by the two Irishmen. Another terrorist moved to the cockpit, to stand over Jessup. He took "Eckstrom's" AK-47.

The giant cargo doors at the rear of the plane opened, and the ramp moved down to touch the ground. The tanker moved into position to begin refueling.

As the tractor jockeyed around and began to back up the ramp into the belly of the plane, a motor-pool Ford arrived. An airman second class jumped out of the driver's seat, a second lieutenant out of the passenger's side. The enlisted man ran around the car and held the rear door for a light colonel. Followed by the lieutenant, the colonel marched up the ramp, holding a clipboard, the twin of the one under Collins's arm.

"Easy now, Major," said the Irishman. "Take a deep breath and swallow. Don't let the butterflies in your stomach carry you away. Think of your family. I'd hate to see them harmed."

The colonel's face was red with the exertion of climbing. Collins was conscious of his own .45, sagging against its belt. It was lighter than those carried by the men behind him. Seven cartridges were missing from its clip.

"Major Collins?" The colonel accepted salutes. "You're late, Major."

Collins swallowed again, working up saliva to speak. "Head winds, Colonel. And the tower had us in a holding pattern for twenty minutes."

The colonel nodded. The lieutenant stood in a military brace. The bogus crew chief supervised as the tractor was hooked to the first line of trailers and moved out. On the ground, it stopped and was unhooked, then maneuvered back up the ramp after another load.

"Bet you're glad to get rid of this cargo,

Major,'' said the colonel. Collins nodded, not trusting himself to speak.

Each trailer held a baby aircraft, the lineal descendants of World War II's buzz bombs. Griffiss Air Force Base was home to the 416th Bombardment Wing, the first in the United States Air Force to go operational with ALCMs—air-launched cruise missiles.

The wings of the missiles were retracted and would remain so until the moment of launching. The cruise missile could amble along at subsonic speeds, its in-flight computer following a terrain-hugging flight plan that permitted the weapon to stay below any effective radar screen. The missile was driven by a small, 150-pound turbofan jet.

In flight, the jet developed 600 pounds of thrust and drove a nuclear warhead with the explosive force of 200,000 tons of TNT—fourteen times the power of the bomb that destroyed Hiroshima. Further, the ALCM in-flight computer carried five target programs, any of which could be selected at the moment of launching. Each missile had a range of 1500 miles and weighed 3,000 pounds. By 1990, 320 of them would be stockpiled at Griffiss.

The colonel, making notes on the board, watched as the second row of trailers was towed out of the plane. Collins handed over his own clipboard on request, and the colonel scribbled his signature as the tractor returned for the third load. The late-afternoon sun barely penetrated the cargo bay, but as the colonel returned Collins's clipboard he took in the marks on Collins's face.

"Get the name of the truck, Major?"

"Pardon, Colonel?" Collins's stomach jumped.

"The one that hit you," the colonel said.

The Irishman laughed. "Joe took a ride on his boy's dirt bike, Colonel. I tried to tell him he's not a kid any longer, but he wouldn't listen."

The colonel nodded, and Collins forced what he hoped would pass as a shamefaced grin.

"None of us are. Well, they're my babies now, we'll take good care of them," the colonel said, motioning to the deadly cargo. "Once I get them tucked away for the night, I'll buy you fellas a drink."

The Irishman stepped in. "We thank you kindly, Colonel, but I'm afraid we'll have to take a rain check. It's Joe's anniversary tomorrow. His wife swore she'd skin me alive if I didn't have him back in time."

"Well, next time, then," said the colonel. "Congratulations, Major. Happy anniversary."

"Thank you," said Collins. "Next time for sure."

He saluted again and the colonel retreated down the ramp. The lieutenant followed. The tractor was maneuvering to join the trailer strings together. The airman held the door for the colonel, then jumped back into the car, which shot toward the distant bunkers, passing the trailers.

Collins sagged, stepping back into the plane, his knees weak with the release of tension.

"That was good, Major," the Irishman said, smiling again. "We're halfway home. Now get us out of here."

Collins started the engines and moved the C-130 through a maze of taxiways, then joined a line of traffic waiting for clearance to take off. There was a delay of fifteen minutes before a runway was available.

The C-130 lumbered down the runway and took off into the gray sky. Collins cleared course with the tower and headed west, until the plane was over Lake Erie, then changed course to the southwest.

Back in the cargo bay, one of the terrorists yelled in triumph. One earphone pulled back, Collins heard them loudly congratulating each other. Their leader seemed annoyed. He sent "Eckstrom" back to quiet them.

Collins strained to hear him over the noise of the engines and the in-flight vibrations of the aircraft.

"We're only halfway home," said the false sergeant. "Save you're celebratin' until we hear how the other men have done."

Others. Collins blinked, wondering what others were involved, wondering what these bastards were going to do with the four nuclear warheads they had stolen.

He glanced at the terrorist leader. "You promised to let them go. My family."

"So I did. Faith, rest your mind, Joe. Seamus Riley's word is his bond."

Despair rocked Collins. He had heard of Seamus Riley. Riley was a bloodthirsty terrorist bastard.

He feared that Jill and the kids were dead.

He thought of the scum terrorizing his family. He thought of rape. He thought of death.

Collins wondered how much longer he had to live.

3

THE BLACK VAN rolled along Peachtree Street, tires hissing against the wet pavement. A storm had passed through thirty minutes earlier.

As night gave way to the early hours of morning, downtown Atlanta was deserted. Streetlights stretched ahead like towering sentinels, while the headlights of an oncoming car peered into the darkness.

"Where in hell are the people?" the driver asked. "A city is supposed to have bloody people livin' in it. It's like comin' in at the end of the world."

"Be happy there are no witnesses," said the man in the passenger seat. "There'll be enough people when we reach the target, Peter."

Peter, the driver, fell silent.

The body of the van was windowless, the sides painted in a seascape mural. The mural's colors were washed out and looked ghostly under the streetlighting. The cab of the van was in darkness, the dashboard lights dimmed.

A traffic light turned red and the driver eased to a stop. The oncoming car approached on the

far side of the intersection. It was a police
cruiser.

"Sweet Jesus, Liam," Peter said nervously.

"Relax."

The light turned green. Van and cruiser
passed each other. Peter's neck ached with the
strain of not turning his head. A moment later,
one eye on his side mirror, he said, "He turned
the corner. He's turnin' to come back."

"Don't panic, Peter," Liam said.

"But we're almost there."

"Just drive on. Drive by. We've time enough.
Seamus made allowance for things like this."

On the van's left were twin office towers,
standing tall. The towers were dark except for
the lobbies and a half dozen office suites.

"The cleaning crews," said Liam, noting the
lights.

Red warning beacons blinked on the roof-
tops. As Peter craned his head skyward, one of
the suites went dark.

"The penthouse is dark, Liam. Where is the
guard?"

"Right where he belongs, in the reception
area. Stop fretting, Peter. We've got the plans.
Seamus knows what he's doing."

The van passed through the next intersection
and barely beat the stoplight. Peter checked the
mirror again. The cruiser, two blocks back,
drove through a red light without stopping.

"He's comin' on. He ran the light."

"Make the next right," Liam said, showing a

calm he did not feel. "Go two blocks and make another. We'll lose him."

Peter obeyed, and by the time he came back onto Peachtree Street there was no sign of the cruiser. Liam glanced back into the van.

"We're almost there," he said to the two terrorists.

The younger one in the back nodded. He crouched against the wall, facing the other man; neither had spoken since entering the van.

Peter turned left onto the street where the office towers were situated.

The glass-walled lobby in each building gave a clear view of anyone inside.

Only one security guard was on duty in the first office building. He was seated at a steel desk beneath a floor-indicator panel, his interest consumed by a 9-inch black-and-white television. The elevators were in a series of short side corridors.

Peter eased the van to the curb near the second office tower and killed the headlights. He shifted into Park but left the engine running.

The driver and the two terrorists in the back were dressed entirely in black: trousers, turtle-necks, sneakers. Black knitted caps covered their hair, and their faces had been darkened with burned cork. Liam, their leader, wore a short brown jacket, with a Western Union patch, over starched gray twill pants and shirt. A .32 Beretta automatic pistol sagged the pocket of the jacket.

Liam climbed out of the van carrying a clipboard, which held a yellow telegram. He then walked boldly to the door.

In the lobby a man ran a polisher over the marble floor, while a guard sat at a desk similar to the one in the other building. The guard held a magazine ten inches from his face. The cleaning man faced away from the approaching terrorist.

Liam found the night bell. The guard jumped but ignored the sound. The cleaning man, deafened by the plug of a pocket radio in his ear and the noise of the polisher, did not hear the ringing of the bell.

The guard did not move. Thirty seconds passed before Liam pressed the bell again. This time he held it down. The guard stood, dropped his magazine, and half-hobbled, half-shuffled to answer the second summons.

He was an old man. His shirt carried a patch for Arden Security Services. He peered through the door, his plastic name tag drooping on its safety pin so that it was unreadable.

Whistling soundlessly and acting bored, Liam held up the clipboard to show him the telegram.

"Open the door."

The guard shook his head but tugged at a ring of keys that was held to his belt by a spring-wound takeup cord. The cleaning man glanced idly over his shoulder but was not interested enough in what was happening to stop what he was doing. He came to the first bank of elevators, turned the corner and disappeared.

The guard inserted a key in a chromed lock at the top of the door and pushed the door open no more than three inches.

"Ain't nobody here, feller. Not this time of night."

"Can't help it. Got a priority telegram here, somebody's got to sign for it. I don't care who."

"Telegram?" He shook his head again. "Who for?"

"Jason something-or-other." Liam held the envelope up to the light, turning away from the door. "Yeah, Jason Leinster at Britamco."

"Mr. Leinster sure as hell ain't here at this time of night, mister."

Muttering, the guard pushed farther through the door as Liam held out clipboard and pen. Before the old man could take either, Liam opened his fingers and clipboard and pen fell, clattering.

The guard cursed. "Clumsy idiot!" He bent automatically to retrieve them. Liam's hand chopped against his neck.

The old man sagged into Liam's hands. He would have fallen to the floor, but he was held up by the cord that was still attached to the key. He was dead, his neck broken by the blow.

Peter's fingers drummed the steering wheel

until he saw Liam strike. He then glanced into the back.

"Now!"

The two men came out the rear doors of the van, the older burdened with an electrician's tool kit. They ran to Liam, who was trying to release the guard's hanging body. The younger terrorist produced a commando knife from a leg sheath. He sliced the cord, which snapped back into its holder, and caught the door before it swung shut on the guard's legs. The three men moved into the lobby, Liam dragging the dead body.

"The man with the polisher, down there," Liam said, pointing.

The young man nodded and ran toward the elevators just as the cleaning man came back into view, still trundling the polisher. He glanced up and stopped in shock as he saw the youth rushing toward him with a knife.

"Who the hell...."

The knife sliced into his belly. The cleaning man made a single strangled noise and let go of the polisher, which whipped around until it banged the wall. He tried to grab the handle of the commando knife, but the terrorist pushed down on the butt, raised the point and yanked the knife upward through muscle tissue and guts. It ripped intestines, spilling blood and gore.

"You...."

It was a question, a curse, a cry of outrage.

The cleaning man was dead even as the word escaped with his last expelled breath. The blade was pulled free and the corpse fell.

The terrorist stooped to wipe his blade on the man's trousers, then glanced around as Liam dragged the dead guard toward the bank of elevators near the desk.

The phony electrician paused at the door to retrieve the clipboard and the pen.

A door at the end of the short corridor opened to reveal a supply closet, where the two bodies were unceremoniously dumped. The "electrician" set his tool kit and the clipboard on the desk then went after the floor polisher, which continued to bump along the wall, banging into and scratching marble panels. He turned off the machine and pushed it into the closet.

Liam checked his watch and shrugged out of the Western Union jacket. He transferred the Beretta to his trousers pocket and threw the jacket into the closet.

His gray shirt bore the Arden Security patch and a plastic name tag that said he was D. Smith.

"Five minutes until the other guard comes back from his rounds."

The trio moved back into the lobby and studied the panels above the elevators. The top eight floors of the building, and the penthouse, housed the offices of Britamco, the corporate name on the phony telegram. A multinational, it was also known as the British-American Corporation.

Little of Britamco's business was transacted within the United Kingdom, but it was still seventy percent British-owned and totally British-controlled.

"Five minutes," repeated the "electrician." He retrieved his tool kit, and the younger man followed him to the fire stairs. Liam sat down at the desk, picking up the abandoned magazine. His eyes flashed each minute to the floor-indicator panel, keeping track of guards and cleaning crew as the elevators moved from floor to floor.

The driver waited at the curb until the three men were safely inside then shifted into gear. He took the offshoot and backed the van down an entrance ramp. From the street, the van was invisible. Only someone walking down the slope would know it was there. The engine idled quietly. Peter shifted into Park again. And there he waited nervously. And as Peter fidgeted, the "electrician" and his partner entered the sub-basement.

LIAM GLANCED AT THE MAGAZINE, idly turning the pages. His ears were intent on the sounds of the building.

Once he turned and looked up at the floor-indicator panels just as the elevator moved from the third floor to the second. A moment later he heard elevator doors open.

A patroling guard stepped off. He was middle-aged and pot-bellied, an ex-cop gone to seed. He carried a time clock slung from one shoulder. He slipped it off as he came into the lobby. He also carried a flashlight.

"Jesus, Charlie, my feet are...."

The complaint broke off as the guard saw Liam.

"Who the hell are you? Where's Charlie?"

Liam quickly produced the Beretta.

"Uh-huh. You're the boss, mister. I don't know what you're after, but I ain't arguing with a gun," the guard said as his flashlight clattered to the floor.

"Turn around," Liam ordered.

"Anything you say."

"Move back to the supply closet."

The guard obeyed. Liam ordered him to open the door. He choked when he saw the two bodies. The front of the cleaning man's clothes were soaked with blood, which had puddled onto the floor.

"Mother of God!"

The Beretta slammed down, and the guard fell on top of the cleaning man's legs. He sagged forward, a moan escaped his lips. Liam hit him again, smashing the Beretta into the guard's brain, then slammed the door against the slumping body. He had killed before, with guns and explosives, but tonight was the first time he had ever killed with his own hands.

It was the first time he had killed a man other than a hated Brit.

He went back to the desk and sat down, breathing harshly. A moment later a car drove by. It was a police cruiser. Liam's thumping heart rose in his chest. "Oh, Christ," he said aloud. "Not now. Not when we're so close to success...."

4

Fog swirled through the London streets, bringing a chill that cut through the warmest clothing. The street was heavily shadowed; every other streetlight had been turned off to conserve energy.

David McCarter turned up the collar of his jacket against the chill and listened to the sounds of the night. Noise was deadened by the fog. He heard the drip, drip of a broken rain gutter, caught the distant clash of gears as a lorry changed speed and heard the soft slide of a leather sole against cobblestones.

McCarter stopped. He was bone weary. He thought longingly of bed, of twelve hours of deep and dreamless sleep. He thought of not having to think, of not having to be alert at every moment. His tiredness was deeper than the bones; it clutched his soul.

He moved onward then stopped again. The man following him was a fraction of a second late in doing the same.

McCarter took inventory. He slipped a hand into his coat and felt the comforting bulk of the Colt Python in its shoulder holster. The Colt, chambered for the .357 Magnum slug, could stop a car. He shrugged his shoulders and felt the length of the sheathed Mark IV commando knife against his spine; he twitched a leg muscle and knew the familiar weight of the ankle gun, and he flexed his fingers, knowing his hands were the most deadly weapons of all.

The fog played tricks with echoes. Where was his tail? Sound suddenly blasted into the night as a window was thrown open, rock music blaring at peak volume from a stereo. It cut off just as suddenly, but in those brief seconds McCarter had moved twenty yards farther and ducked into a shadowed doorway.

He waited, listening. The footsteps sounded, running, the tail fearing he had lost him. David strained to see, then shrank back as a dark shape loomed out of the fog. The shape was coming straight toward him, arm held out, hand pointing a weapon. McCarter forgot his guns, forgot the knife. When the runner was only three paces away, he stepped out from the doorway....

McCarter opened his eyes and blinked. The dream, the nightmare, was still vivid. Cold sweat had formed on his forehead.

The girl who shared his bed was in a deep sleep, although it was the middle of the day. Her mouth was open. Her breathing was harsh, exaggerated.

The room was as dark as night; the heavy

draperies completely shut out the light of day. David listened, muscles and nerves tight with tension.

Suddenly the girl snorted, then flopped onto her back. Her hand fell across David's hip, and he flinched. His breath caught in his throat, and he listened even more attentively.

Something had awakened him.

Someone was in the room.

The flash of light as the intruder had opened the door and ducked inside had awakened him. Now he waited for his eyes to adjust to the darkness.

A black patch shifted, taking a step away from the door. The deep-piled carpeting muffled any sound.

McCarter blinked his eyes until they adjusted to the darkness. He lay facing the door, his right arm on top of the bedcovers.

He caught the musky odor of a man's cologne or after-shave.

It was not his brand.

Yet it was familiar.

The black patch shifted again. The intruder took two more steps then stopped just out of arm's reach of the bed.

McCarter's eyes could differentiate shades of darkness. He could make out that the intruder wore light clothing.

McCarter shifted his left foot slightly, drawing it up a few inches, ready to spring. He let a whistling breath escape his mouth, his head lolling toward the girl, and then five seconds later lolling back again while his free hand came up, flopped back.

The intruder froze, not moving for a count of sixty seconds. David tried to judge his size: six-two or -three, about 180 pounds.

The intruder moved, reaching out with both hands.... McCarter launched himself from the bed. He hit the man in the belly with his shoulder. The intruder grunted in surprise and fell back. McCarter followed, but a foot tangled in the bedding brought him down.

The girl sat up and screamed.

McCarter went after the intruder as the man rolled away, scrabbling on his hands and fighting to free his foot from the bedcovers, which had followed him onto the floor. He snagged fingers into the other's belt, felt canvas. McCarter ducked as the intruder slammed an elbow back. He reached up and grabbed the man's collar as he tried to scramble to his feet, slamming his free knee into the small of the man's back.

The other groaned and fell heavily, but McCarter's doubled leg took most of the dead-weight. He crooked an arm around the intruder's neck and used his other hand to lever his forearm against the intruder's chin.

The man grunted again and tried to smash the back of his skull against McCarter's face. They rolled, thrashing, as the intruder fought to break the hold that was choking his breath. The girl was shrieking now, short sobbing cries that came as quickly as she could gulp air.

"McCarter! Damn you, leave off!"

The voice was a rasp, but the use of McCarter's name made him hesitate just as he was ready to deliver the killing stroke. He rolled the man onto his belly and straddled him.

"The drapes!" McCarter said. What the hell was her name? "For Christ's sake, Mavis, open the drapes. Turn on a light. And leave off the bloody bawling."

The shrieks stopped, although she continued to snuffle as she fumbled for the lamp.

McCarter blinked against the soft light and recognized the man beneath him.

"Simms! You asshole. You ruddy bastard."

"Let me up, Sergeant. Damn it, give off."

McCarter released Simms's arm, rolled back and came to his feet. Major Geoffrey Simms sat up, rubbing the wrist of an injured arm. He wore starched khakis with the pips of his rank on the shoulder straps; the black beret of the SAS was rolled and tucked under one strap. He wore paratrooper's jump boots, polished to a gleam that threw back highlights from the lamp, and on his shoulder was the SAS patch.

The SAS had been McCarter's outfit before he switched his allegiance to Phoenix Force. The SAS was the elite special army force that was Britain's last line of defense against terrorist activities.

As commanding officer of McCarter's company, Major Geoffrey Simms had prompted him to apply for the unknown assignment that led to his selection for Phoenix Force. They had clashed almost from the moment of Simms's arrival, two men whose dislike for one another was returned in full measure.

Ignoring his own nakedness, McCarter went to the suitcase that stood open on a stand against the wall and came out with the Colt Python. He turned and pointed it toward Simms while the major dusted off his clothes. When Simms looked up and saw the gun, he froze again.

"You don't need that, Sergeant. This is an official visit."

"I'm not in your bloody company now, Simms."

"There's still a spot on our organizational chart marked with your name and rank, Sergeant. 'On detached service.' But still in Her Majesty's armed services."

"But not subject to your orders."

Simms blinked. "That's not why I'm here. I came to give you a message—some friends of yours have been trying to call you, but you don't answer."

McCarter's eyes shot to the pager on top of the dresser, laid out beside his wallet and the contents of his pockets. He could see that the green signal light was off. He walked to the dresser and picked it up. The pager's switch was properly in the On position.

"Bloody batteries," he said. Had it been working this morning when he checked into the hotel? He could not remember, and that was enough to worry him.

He should not have been that tired.

His life depended on staying alert, on knowing at all times what was happening around him, so that when the moment of action came he would be ready.

"All right, Simms. You delivered the message. Now get out."

"Not yet. I was told to deliver you to a secure telephone, so get dressed and let's get moving."

"What the hell's goin' on?" cried the woman, clutching the retrieved sheet to her nakedness. "Bloody men breakin' into a person's room! Who is this sod?"

McCarter scooped her clothes from a chair and threw them at her, aware of the smirk on Simms's face. Hatred distorted McCarter's face. He dropped the Colt into the suitcase.

"Get dressed, Mavis. It's time to go home."

"The name is Clara," the woman said indignantly, but she retreated into the bathroom, clothes clutched in front of her.

"Why you, Simms?" McCarter asked, getting dressed.

"Why not me?" asked Simms, grinning without humor.

McCarter knew Simms had taken on the errand himself, although it would have been just as simple to phone the hotel and tell McCarter to get in touch with Stony Man. Any flunky on a desk could have done it.

Simms wanted this meeting. He wanted a chance to take McCarter unaware. He had been waiting for this for a long time; David knew with a certainty that he would be dead if Simms had come out the winner.

But Simms had lost, and in losing he had quickly taken advantage of his official errand. The bastard. McCarter stepped into his trousers, buttoned his shirt.

"Hurry up in there, Mavis!" he called.

"It's Clara!" she said again, tugging at her skirt as she came out. She left the room with a flounce that made Simms chuckle.

"Just your type, Sergeant."

"Do you have a type, Simms?"

Simms flushed, his eyes narrowing. "You'd better pack while you're at it. I don't think you'll be coming back."

McCarter had expected as much. So much for his R&R. Stony Man would not have called him out for anything less than the utmost in importance.

He was ready. Everything McCarter possessed fit into the one suitcase, his traveling kit and a thin leather attaché case. He strapped the suitcase and picked it up as Simms opened the door.

The hotel lobby was busy, but the staff ignored McCarter as he left the building, following Simms. A driver and car waited.

They drove through heavy afternoon traffic and at last arrived at an army base near Brixton. They were scrutinized carefully by armed guards, before the car was allowed to proceed through the gate. They were scrutinized again by a guard in front of a building marked Communications, and by a young lieutenant at a desk within.

The identity card McCarter presented had his correct name but otherwise had no bearing with the reality of his service, either with Her Majesty's armed forces or with Phoenix Force. He did not allow Simms to see it. The credentials were accepted without question, and a third guard used a plastic ID of his own to electronically unlock a steel door that was heavy enough for a vault.

"Sergeant."

McCarter turned back as the door swung open by itself.

"One of these days you'll be back in my country, Sergeant," said Simms, his face set. "Matters will be different then."

"A fair fight, Simms? Like today?"

"Any way you wish, Sergeant."

"Forget it, Simms. The SAS is one of the best elite fighting forces on this bloody planet and *you* are a damn disgrace to that force. I'd take you on anywhere, anytime, but I really don't want to get my hands dirty on shit like you."

Before Simms could say more, McCarter stepped into the room and the door closed.

It was a gray room, ten feet square with walls, ceiling and floor lined with metal. The room held only a small gray steel desk, a single gray steel straight-backed chair and a red telephone with a scrambling device.

McCarter sat in the chair and picked up the instrument. The receiver crackled loudly, the connection already made.

He spoke and the scrambler tore his voice apart, shredding it then sending the sounds to a communications satellite that carried only military and government traffic. The shreds were bounced to an earth station on the other side of the Atlantic and fed to Stony Man Farm, where a duplicate scrambler telephone pieced them together in the proper order. There was a slight distortion caused by the process of disassembly and reassembly, but McCarter's voice came through with clarity.

He spoke first to the duty man in Stony Man's own communication center. Ten seconds later, he was talking to Colonel Yakov Katzenelenbogen.

5

THE AFTERNOON LIGHT was fading fast when the C-130 took to the air on its return flight to the southwest. The plane was still over western Pennsylvania, lumbering along in its slow airspeed, when the night descended.

The plane was on autopilot. Collins dozed, waking only to acknowledge a radio call when the C-130 passed from one air-traffic-control center to another.

The evening died as the plane passed over Ohio, Tennessee, the Ozarks. Seven hours had slipped away when Seamus Dolan Riley touched Collins's shoulder, and the pilot woke with a start.

"Huh?"

"We're there, Major."

Blinking, Collins rubbed grit from his eyes and peered through the windshield and then the side window. The land below was dark. Overhead the sky was solidly overcast, nothing broke the blackness except the lights of the instrument panel.

By day the land below was not quite a desert,

but useless to men. By night it was like a cold corner of hell.

"Take us down," Riley said.

"Down there?" Collins shook his head. "You're out of your mind."

"I'm quite sane. There will be lights," he assured.

A glimmer of light suddenly appeared and turned into a line of orange as men raced along the ground, touching fire to kerosene torches. The line doubled, although at this altitude it seemed no longer than a pencil and scarcely as wide.

Collins switched off the autopilot and resumed manual control. The plane banked, lost altitude as it slipped to one side and moved around in a wide circle. Collins knew a ring of low hills surrounded the strip of ground that this maniac expected him to land on.

"It's crazy," he said. "Maybe with a small plane, a Cessna or a Cub, but there's no way I can take this thing down without an instrument approach, without a tower to talk me in."

"Do your best, Major," said Riley. He smiled. "I'm putting my trust and my life in your flying skills."

The C-130 continued to lose altitude, disappearing from the radar screens of the local traffic-control center. Near the edge of the screen, and about to be handed over to the next station, the overworked and understaffed center never noticed its departure.

It was crazy, Collins thought as he lined up the plane on the double row of flares. The airstrip still seemed too narrow to accept the plane. Why was he doing anything to help these bastards? They were not going to let him walk away. And his family. . . .

But hope refused to die. They would live.

The wheels fell with a solid clunk. The instrument panel showed green. He cut back on the airspeed, lowered the flaps and angled the nose of the plane between the flickering torches.

The wheels touched sooner than he expected, jolting everyone on the plane. Collins fought the wheel and threw the engines into reverse as the C-130 jarred its way across a pockmarked, pot-holed concrete airstrip.

This was the second landing the plane had made at this place, this day. The airstrip was a part of an abandoned World War II fighter training base.

In the darkness Collins could not see the crumbling Quonset hangar that still stood. In the daytime, fire-blackened ruins remained where the operations building had once stood. Of the barracks and service buildings, only ragged foundations were left.

To Collins's surprise that morning, a wind sock fluttered from a rough pole at the end of the runway. It had been raised two years earlier by drug smugglers. DEA agents had been waiting when the smugglers' first plane landed. The strip had been left untouched since.

This was where Seamus Riley had drawn his gun on an unsuspecting Jessup, after earlier forcing Collins to take him aboard in place of Brownlow, who was unknown to any of the regular crew. Riley had forced Collins to land at the erstwhile training base, then his men had joined him.

After landing, the crew had been ordered out, where they had been greeted by the armed terrorists. One team of terrorists had quickly swapped places with the crew, while another swarmed into the cargo bay and removed a warhead from every third missile.

The terrorists were prepared. The stolen warheads were replaced by dummies, the shrouds tied down and the seals renewed. The entire operation, from landing to takeoff, took thirty-three minutes. And only Collins and Jessup remained of the original crew when the C-130 took to the air again.

Now the plane bumped to a halt at the very end of the line of torches, less than fifty feet from the end of the airstrip. The terrorists undogged the hatch while the original crew was brought from the hangar, a stumbling, shuffling line of confused men.

"What's the matter with my men?" Collins demanded as the first few were shoved aboard.

"They've been drugged," said Riley. "It makes them easier to control."

"Bastard!" Collins said, slumping in his seat. "Bastards!"

A few of the men were able to board the plane under their own power. The others were cursed at, cuffed and thrown inside.

"Eckstrom" came forward and ordered Jessup to stand. The lieutenant was frozen in his seat.

"Move, damn you!" He prodded Jessup with his Kalashnikov.

"The lad is paralyzed with fear," Riley said. "Get a couple of the boys to help you."

Two of the terrorists grabbed Jessup's arms and yanked him to his feet. They tore his flight suit down from his shoulder, while a third drove a needle through the fabric of his shirt.

The drug worked quickly, racing into his bloodstream. Collins watched as Jessup sagged and fell back into his seat.

"Bastards!" Collins said again.

The trio turned their attention to him. One terrorist clubbed Collins with the butt of his .45, while the others grabbed him. Using the Kalashnikov, "Eckstrom" began smashing the instruments.

"No!" cried Collins. "Stop him!"

"Easy, lads," said Riley as a needle stabbed into Collins's arm. "He has to be able to fly the aircraft."

Collins's dose was smaller, but the injection was given roughly—as though the terrorist was venting all of his anger in the attack. For an instant Collins thought the needle would break off in his arm. Pain stabbed and turned into a screaming ache. A rush of heat flooded his body.

"My wife!" he said, his tongue thickening. "My children! Damn you. You said you'd let them go!"

"Ah." Riley rubbed his nose with a finger. "Your family. Think of this as war, Major. In every war it is tragic but accepted that civilians suffer a higher percentage of casualties than the armies involved."

Collins tried to speak, but he could not force the words from his throat. He caught the back of his seat, slumped into it, no longer able to stand under his own power.

One of the terrorists instructed his fellow guncocks to get off the plane. The real Eckstrom's body had been loaded with the crew. Riley turned to Collins again.

"Major, when the last of my men are off, you will have three minutes to get this aircraft into the air. After that, my men will open fire. This is your only chance to save your crew."

Collins was stoned, his mind anchored in deep fog. He stared numbly at the wrecked instrument panel, and with an effort he turned his head to stare at the unconscious Jessup. Through blurring eyes he was aware of the departure of the terrorists. He also heard the slam of the hatch.

Scum. Filthy murdering scum. *I should have flown the plane into the ground, with them on it,* Collins thought.

Acting by instinct, Collins's hand moved to the throttle. The engines revved, roaring and kicking up dust. The galvanized-steel trash cans that held the kerosene fires sent tongues of orange flame whipping across the airstrip, close to the ground.

The band of Irish terrorists, standing with guns ready, watched as the big plane slowly turned and began to move. The engines roared again as Collins fed them full throttle. And, at what seemed the last possible instant, the wheels lost touch with the ground. The terrorists ran along the row of fires, clamping lids back onto the trash cans as the C-130 cleared the ring of low hills.

A Mayflower moving van appeared out of the darkness of the hangar, only its parking lights lit. The terrorists stripped out of the stolen Air Force uniforms as the van moved slowly along the edge of the runway, gathering them aboard.

Riley took a pair of white coveralls with the Mayflower logo on one breast, the name "Jack" embroidered on the other. He pulled the .45 from its holster and thrust the bundle of clothing into the back of the van. He swung onto the step of the moving vehicle and climbed into the cab.

"Let's get away from here."

They could hear the plane in the darkness as it flew beyond the hills, barely above tree level. Riley relaxed as the van turned away from the airstrip and moved onto a narrow country road.

"Michael, I've a most killing thirst."

The driver handed over a pint of whiskey. Riley uncapped the bottle and took a deep drink. He sighed with pleasure at the bite of the liquor, then wiped the back of his hand across his mouth. He capped the bottle.

"Now that restores the soul."

"How long do you think it will take before the substitution is discovered, Seamus?"

"Now that depends on how successful the rest of the men are this night, and on how thorough an inspection they make when they discover the plane's missing."

"Do you really think the phony warheads will fool them?"

"They'll fool a casual look, thanks to the trace elements included. But once the authorities find the wreckage of the plane and check out Collins's house, they'll know something is very wrong. By that time it will make no difference."

"It seems a shame, takin' only four of the warheads."

"You're a greedy man, you are, Michael McGinnity. Four is enough. We'll have our fortune and win our war with this lot, or not at all. Now let's be away from this place before a stray sheriff's patrol wonders what good Irish lads are doin' here this time of night."

Michael turned on the headlights as Riley uncapped the pint and took another drink. Five miles farther, the narrow road intersected a major highway. The van turned east. Eventually it would head north, toward a base less than one hundred miles from Rome, New York, where the day's charade had been played out.

The warheads had gone on ahead, transported on another truck. By now they had reached their destination and were being converted to more flexible weapons by the terrorist organization's technicians. If the other teams were successful in their missions, the warheads would be ready when needed.

Seamus Riley was satisfied with the day's work.

HEADING NORTHWEST of its original flight plan, beneath the radar coverage that might bring it back onto the screens of the air-traffic controllers, the C-130 floundered under Collins's uncertain hand.

Collins swallowed against the metallic taste of the drug and fumbled for the autopilot; but it had been smashed. His hand fell back. He could not remember what he was doing or where he was. Suddenly both hands dropped from the yoke and he fell sideways, his head lolling.

The plane shuddered under the change and nosed downward. It remained airborne until fifty miles west of the abandoned base, where the angle of descent carried it into the base of a hill.

The crash site was twenty miles from the closest population center, ten miles from the nearest road. The fireball was seen only by a

Navaho sheepherder who paused outside of his shack to stare until the glow had faded.

Two hundred miles to the southwest, firemen picked through the glowing embers that had been Collins's house. The fire had been out for hours, but the rubble was still too hot to approach the cellar.

"You really think they're in there, Chief?" asked Collins's closest neighbor.

The fire chief shrugged. "Wife's car is in the garage. The children missed school today. Didn't tell anybody they were going away...."

"Really a shame," said the neighbor. "They were nice people. What a way to die. I wonder if they knew what hit them?"

"I hope not," said the chief, compassionately.

Another hour passed before the C-130 was reported overdue and presumed missing. By that time the moving van had crossed the state line.

6

LIAM NERVOUSLY CHEWED HIS LOWER LIP as the police cruiser moved slowly past the twin office towers, the police scanning each lobby. Liam pretended to be scanning his magazine until the cruiser passed from view. When the car left his sight, he quickly drew the Beretta and concealed it under the desk.

Minutes passed before the police car appeared on the far side of the building, moving as slowly as before. It did not stop.

Liam's breath escaped in a rush as the cruiser turned back onto Peachtree Street. He brought the Beretta into the open, his hand trembling, and restored the gun to his pocket. Soon after, the two terrorists returned from the fire stairs. The "electrician" beamed.

"It was easy, Liam. Like takin' candy from a kid. A child could cross-wire their alarm system."

Liam checked his watch. "We've got eighteen minutes until the guard is scheduled to clock in again."

"Plenty of time." Things were going just as Riley had predicted; the "electrician" felt good.

He produced the ring of keys that had belonged to the old guard. He sorted through the lot, choosing one that fitted the elevator-control panel. He opened the panel and killed the lights.

Digging into his kit, the "electrician" produced gas masks, for himself and his partner, and a flashlight. Further digging produced four grenades; his partner took two, balancing the deadly weights in his hand.

The two men squatted and put their grenades on the floor while they put on the masks. When they stood, they moved to the elevator that serviced Britamco exclusively.

The door opened when the button was pushed, but the cab of the elevator was dark. The "electrician" clipped a grenade to his belt, pulling up his shirt on that side to leave it free, and switched on the flashlight as he stepped inside. The younger terrorist followed and pressed the button for the penthouse.

The elevator accelerated at express speed. The "electrician" switched off the flashlight. The youth pulled the pin on one of his grenades. The doors opened.

Beyond was a foyer. Opposite was a glass wall and a single glass door with a bronze handle.

The two men took in the scene quickly. Beyond the glass wall was a reception area. At the desk a security guard, dressed in the brown uniform of Britamco, wore a .38 Police Positive in a belt holster.

The guard looked up in surprise and started

to rise as a grenade rolled from the darkness and came to rest at the base of the door. The terrorists flattened themselves against the corners of the elevator cab as the grenade exploded.

The glass door and wall had cracked under the blast but had not broken; the door had bowed inward and popped free of the locking bolts. It hung at a crazy angle, the lower hinge broken.

The explosion had blown the guard to the floor behind the desk. He groaned and tried to pick himself up as the "electrician" pulled the pin on his grenade and tossed it through the opening.

There was a pop, the terrorists automatically ducking back, and gas hissed into the reception area. The guard shook his head. He breathed in the first wisp of gas and collapsed, dead.

The terrorists moved through the broken door, through the cloud of gas, and entered the corridor. The penthouse contained Britamco's executive offices.

The two men ignored the doors on either side of the corridor and did not stop until they reached the door at the end. It was not locked. The "electrician" pushed through and entered the office of Britamco's director of operations for the United States.

The office was larger than many two-bedroom condominiums. It seemed underfurnished because of its size. An ornate fireplace with an Adams mantel stood against one wall, while on another was a Rosa Bonheur horse in a gilt frame. Draperies were pulled back from glass walls that met at the corner of the building. The city of Atlanta lay revealed beyond.

The "electrician" produced an envelope from an inner pocket and placed it on the Chippendale table that served as a desk.

"That's it," he said. "Let's go."

They left as quickly as they had come, reaching the lobby in time to hear the sharp clamor of a telephone. It was in a panel beneath the floor indicator.

"One of the cleaning crews," Liam said. "They're ready to move, and they want to know why the elevator lights are out."

Ignoring the clamor, the "electrician" opened the panel and turned the lights back on while Liam dug a walkie-talkie from the tool kit and pressed the transmit button three times. In the van Peter caught the signal and drove up the ramp.

All three terrorists ran toward the van. Liam tore off the Arden Security shirt. Beneath it he wore a multicolored T-shirt.

Peter hit the headlights, and the van took the corner back onto Peachtree Street.

"Slow down!" Liam said sharply. "We don't want to be stopped now, for God's sake."

Peter slowed down and checked the side mirror. The street was no longer empty. Ahead, a street sweeper lumbered through an intersection. Light traffic began to appear.

Peter drove carefully for eight blocks, turned into the parking lot of a small shopping center.

He parked near several public telephones. Liam got out and walked to the phones. He lifted a receiver and punched out the number. After three rings, a sleepy voice answered.

"Hello?"

"Jason Leinster?"

"Who is this? Hello?"

"Jason?" A woman's voice overflowed in the background. "Who is it, Jason? What's it about?"

"Christ, if you'd shut up maybe I could find out," Leinster said. "Who is this? Jesus. It's a quarter to five—it's the middle of the night!"

"No questions, Leinster. Tell me, how could a man with a name as proud as yours work for the Brits?"

"Is this a gag? Who the hell are you?"

"Listen, Leinster and listen well. There is a letter on your desk. Go to your office and read it. Read it, and act upon it."

"What? Wait a damn minute. . . ."

Liam held down the cutoff lever and replaced the handset in the cradle. Only then did he permit himself a sigh as tension left his body.

For his team, the night's work was done.

AT THE SAME HOUR other teams were on the move, wrapping up similar missions, each directed against one of the fifty largest British-owned or British-controlled operations in the United States.

In each raid there had been violence: people had died—some brutally, sadistically, some without knowing what had hit them. Liam felt regret for the deaths, but he knew they were necessary. Seamus Riley had emphasized that point to the soldiers in his private army.

"They won't take us seriously unless they're hurting. Unless they feel pain," Seamus had said.

"But Americans, Seamus," several had protested. "The factions have agreed to keep the States safe ground. We need their money and their arms."

"When this is done," Riley said, "we'll have all the money we'll ever need. The bloody world is a supermarket for all of the guns and tanks and missile launchers we'll need to drive out the Brits. Ireland will be united—our way and no other. The Americans be damned; we've waited long enough for justice."

Riley's face was flushed with anger and enthusiasm.

"We'll have the bomb, and when we do, what has gone on these past twenty years will seem a Sunday-school picnic. They'll listen. They'll have to listen."

LIAM RETURNED TO THE VAN. Peter shifted into gear again.

Twenty minutes later, the van was returned to

the suburban street from which it had been taken. There had been brief stops to dispose of the stolen license plates and the equipment used during the raid.

Later the younger terrorist arrived in a cab at the Trailways bus station, and the "electrician" had returned to the room he had been renting. At eight o'clock he would return his pickup truck and tools to the small firm that had hired him two weeks earlier and announce that he was quitting. Later today he would be on a plane to Los Angeles. Following a circuitous route, by tomorrow afternoon he would be in New York City. Peter would be in Chicago, flying directly on the first flight that morning.

Liam waited at the motel until 6:00 A.M., then crossed the street to a coffee shop to make another phone call, this time long distance. He had the correct change ready, dropped it into the slot at the operator's command. The phone rang three times. He held down the cutoff lever, dialed again, fed coins again. This time it was picked up after the first ring, and he said one word.

"Atlanta."

The man on the other end hung up, and the dial tone sounded.

The night's work was complete.

7

SEVENTY MINUTES after being roused from his sleep, Jason Leinster slumped behind his Chippendale table, his flesh clammy with fear. The glass walls of the office showed the flush of dawn.

Leinster had dressed hastily. His shirt hung out the back of his trousers, and his cheeks were stubbled with unshaven beard. His full head of white hair stood in untidy tufts, where he had nervously run his fingers through it.

"It's crazy!" he said.

The office was crowded with FBI agents and police.

Teams of homicide detectives were busy in the reception area of the penthouse, while below in the lobby, others waited for the medical examiner to finish a cursory examination of the bodies. He stood, dusting his trousers at the knee, and said, "Okay, take them away."

The ME headed for the nearest elevator that would take him to the penthouse. Other technicians had already photographed the carnage, dusted the desks, the chairs, the elevators, the discarded magazine. The cleaning crews had been gathered on another floor and were being interrogated, although they had seen nothing, heard nothing.

There were camera crews as well, from the Atlanta television stations, and teams of newspaper reporters and radio newsmen.

The incident in Atlanta was not the first story to break. The wire services had already logged reports about a dozen terrorist raids, although no one had connected them as part of a single over-all attack. The reporters waited like bloodhounds for scraps of fresh information.

There were horror-thirsty gawkers, a hundred or more, drawn to the scene of tragedy by the wail of sirens. Barricades held them back, and uniformed police checked credentials of those who claimed to work in the building.

"Crazies," Leinster said, glancing at the letter one of the FBI men held by the corners, although it had already been dusted for prints that did not exist. Only Leinster's fingers had marked the paper.

"Five million dollars!" he said. "They're out of their minds."

The letter was typed in capital letters with an oversized typeface, on paper that bore the heading THE PEOPLE'S REPUBLIC OF IRELAND. The same inscription appeared on the envelope. There was no address, no other means of identification.

The FBI agent read the letter.

To the British-American Corporation, Ltd.:

You have been judged and found guilty of high crimes against the Irish people.

As compensation to your victims, you are herewith ordered to give the sum of five million dollars ($5,000,000) U.S., payable to the account of the People's Republic of Ireland, Banque Nationale, Tripoli, Libya.

As proof and evidence of the power of the courts of the People's Republic of Ireland, within seventy-two hours of receiving this letter, the Army of the Republic will destroy a major British-owned or British-controlled property within the United States.

After that event, you will be given twenty-four hours to complete transfer of the money. Failure to comply will lead to the destruction of additional British property.

By your acts know that you have declared yourselves an enemy of the Irish people. As your enemy, we, the people of Ireland, shall not hesitate to use the weapon of God's ultimate justice to punish transgressors and their transgressions.

Our cause is noble, our hearts steadfast. Our souls are committed to the war for Irish liberation.

We are the army of God's fury.

We are the Fury Bomb.

"A bunch of maniacs," Leinster said. "What else can they be?"

"Crazies, maybe," said the FBI agent, "but there are four dead bodies here that indicate we'd better listen to what they're saying."

"And give them the five million?" cried Leinster, outraged. "These Irish bastards aren't the only crazies around here!"

As MADNESS SWEPT ATLANTA and other major cities in the United States, well-trained, calm, professional people—known to Hal Brognola and the crew at Stony Man Farm as "sources"—were updating the men who worked at the largest, most intricate and the damn best antiterrorist center in the entire world.

Hal and the Stony Man crew were assimilating the information given to them and planning, plotting their course of action. In Brognola's mind, the course was simple.

"Get me Phoenix Force," he growled.

8

FOUR MEN AND A WOMAN were in the War Room at Stony Man Farm.

Computer wizard Aaron "The Bear" Kurtzman sat in front of a CRT console, his hands resting on the computer's keyboard.

His eyes took in the green glare of the screen and the other persons in the room: April Rose, Gary Manning, Yakov Katzenelenbogen and Hal Brognola.

Katz, the senior member of Phoenix Force—a man with one arm missing, blasted off during the Six Day War—sat erect in a chair, a cane at his side. He leaned forward, his face drawn. The veteran fighter seemed tired.

April sat beside Katz, Manning beside her. Hal stood and paced as The Bear accessed the machine.

"Got it," Kurtzman said. A list of company names came up on the screen. Brognola began to read the list aloud.

"British Petroleum. Cunard Lines. Intercontinental Trading Corporation. Hayes-Eastwood Stores. Royal Dutch Shell. Lloyds Bank of California...." The list seemed endless. "Arden

Security Services," said Brognola. "They're nationwide."

"They hire winos and bums," said Manning, "college boys—whoever they can get for minimum wage."

"They didn't do much for their parent company, Britamco," said Hal.

The list continued.

Yakov thumped his cane on the floor. The others glanced at him.

"I think we're getting carried away. There are thousands of these little companies. The letters threaten a major property. Cut out everything with a value of less than a million dollars."

Kurtzman touched the keyboard and the screen cleared. His fingers danced and the program began again, from the beginning, but this time much of the underbrush had been cleared away. Still, the program took ten minutes to run.

"Over seven hundred possibles remain," said Yakov. "How do we find the one they're going to hit?"

"And how much time do we have?" asked Hal. "The various letters said within seventy-two hours, but that gives them a lot of leeway."

"They want publicity as well as money," said Gary. "Otherwise, why hit so many companies in one operation? I think they'll give the story time to build to the maximum."

"Cocky bastards," said Hal. "We've pulled out all the stops. We have full cooperation right down the line from the FBI and the various state and local police agencies. Already there must be ten thousand police and other agencies working on tracing the attack teams.''

''Has it been cleared with the Man?'' asked Gary.

''Personally,'' said Hal. ''He's been on the phone half the morning. Justice and Defense are on full alert and the National Guard commanders in all fifty states have put their troops on standby.''

It was 11:00 A.M. At that moment David McCarter was over the Irish Channel.

By then, reports from Stony Man sources had come in from all of the targets of the raids. Not all raids had been as successful as the one in Atlanta. Brognola updated Gary and Yakov while waiting for the computer to be accessed for its next task.

''In Chicago, the terrorist team was intercepted by a police patrol car that was able to call in reinforcements. They took out the whole team, all three men, but police suffered heavy casualties doing it.''

''All three dead?'' asked Gary.

''Unfortunately. The terrorists wouldn't surrender. The last one blew himself apart with a grenade. We have pictures and prints on the other two. All had Irish accents, so pictures and prints are being rushed to both police and military agencies in England and in Ireland. Maybe they'll make something of them.''

"No trace on the terrorists in the other cities?" Gary asked.

"Nothing," said Hal. "It's incredible, but somehow between a hundred and two hundred foreigners, who would stand out in any crowd, managed to vanish into thin air."

"What's being done?" asked Yakov.

"Full coverage of public transportation, airports, bus terminals, train stations. A sweep of every hotel, motel, tourist camp and rooming house that accept transients in the target cities. It's amazing how many first-generation Irish are in this country, and the number of them living in hotels and rooming houses. But so far there's nothing to tie any of them to the raiders. The outcries are starting to come in from Irish nationalists and civil rights organizations, screaming Nazi-Fascist dictatorship because we're even looking for the terrorists."

"When the fire bombs start coming through their windows, they'll have something else to scream about," Gary said sourly. "What about this People's Republic of Ireland?"

"Another blank. We're pushing our informants, here and across the water, but it's something new."

Except for the company and the amount demanded, the letters had been the same in every instance. A few asked for one or two million, a few at the top end demanded ten million. The total came to one hundred eighty million dollars.

"Seldom do you see a terrorist organization this well organized," Hal informed them.

"They could have government help. That's a possibility to be kept in mind," said Yakov. "But I don't think even our old friend in Libya would try anything quite like this, even though the money is to be deposited in one of his banks."

Brognola said, "I agree with the colonel. I could see a band of criminals trying to extort from a single company, but nothing on this scale. Still, considering what has happened thus far, it's been agreed that we have to take their demands seriously."

"Have any companies agreed to pay?" asked Gary.

"Not yet. They're still talking it over. But I don't think they will; not unless the terrorists carry out their threat to destroy a major property."

Most of the six hours since the first threats had been reported had been used in organizing the investigation. Using forces put in motion by Brognola, Gary had caught a Canadian Armed Forces jet to Andrews Air Force Base. From there, a helicopter brought him directly to Stony Man. He had arrived thirty minutes earlier.

"McCarter was in London," said Hal. "Right at hand, as it were, so he's working over there."

"That could be bad news," Gary said.

"Very bad," added Yakov. "It's bad luck

David was there. He's the worst possible choice to go into the snake pit. As soon as he opens his mouth every third person he sees will want to shoot him.''

"Maybe," Brognola said, "but there wasn't anything else we could do. Remember, there are already more than a hundred bodies; we're in a shooting war. There was no time to send someone from this side of the water, even if Ohara and Encizo had been available.''

Keio and Rafael were still on standby, awaiting developments, waiting to see on what front the main battle would be fought.

"Let's get this list broken down by region," April said.

Kurtzman tapped out the new request, and the printer beside the computer console began to click, spilling folded paper into the document receptacle. When the noise stopped, Gary ripped away the printout and scanned the list. He shook his head in disgust.

"There are a dozen possibles within twenty miles of Washington, a hundred between here and New York.''

"The fuel depots and refineries along the Jersey shore," said Hal.

"They're on the list," said Gary.

"Spectacular," said Yakov. "Perhaps too spectacular.''

"But the security is lousy," said Gary. "Two or three men could go through those fences like water through cheesecloth. If they want to make that much noise."

"British consulates," said April Rose. The men looked at her. "They're not on the list, but they could be targets."

"I hope not," said Yakov. "If we have to include cultural and governmental sites, there's no hope of covering them all."

"Besides," said Hal, "only the most dedicated Marxist would consider the British government industry-controlled."

"But aren't they?" April asked. "Marxist, I mean. Look at the name they chose—the People's Republic. That's straight from the textbook. It's well-known that the IRA and its splinter offshoots are Marxist."

"A brilliant thought," said Yakov. "But again, I have to hope you're wrong."

"We have to cut away the deadwood," Hal said.

Gary continued to study the printout, scanning back and forth. Twice he stopped at a name, went on, came back and locked on it.

The information was scant, merely a corporate subsidiary and an address. He tapped the printout, musing.

"Something?" said Yakov.

"Maybe. A hunch."

Yakov and the other Phoenix Force men had learned to trust Gary's hunches.

"Ames Computronics, Sussex, New Jersey."

"Sussex is about as far northwest as you can

get and still be in New Jersey," said Kurtzman. He punched up a regional map. "Near Milford, Pennsylvania and Port Jervis, New York. There's a private landing strip at Sussex and another at Port Jervis. Nearest Air Force base is Middletown, New York, forty miles farther. The Sussex strip can take Lear jets."

April turned to Gary. "The helicopter trip would take a good two hours."

"I think Ames Computronics in Sussex is the company they're going to hit. I'll go over alone—we can't afford to spread ourselves thin. Lay on a Lear at Andrews," said Gary, moving toward the door; he dropped the printout on a table.

Minutes were precious. Even if the terrorists milked as much suspense as possible from their threat, less than sixty-six hours remained.

"I'll patch you in with the New Jersey State Police and with the FBI out of Newark," said April, as Gary reached the door. "Someone will meet you at Sussex."

She picked up the telephone and called the alert shack where the chopper pilots waited. By the time Gary arrived, his chopper would be ready to take off.

"Let's get this list on the wire," said Hal, shuffling papers into his briefcase. "I've got to get back to the White House to give the Man a face-to-face report. You'll coordinate here, Colonel?"

"For the moment," Yakov said broodingly.

"At least we'll get a firsthand look at security around the targets," said Hal.

"'We are the fury bomb,'" said Yakov. "What do you suppose it means?"

"Rhetoric," said Hal. "Terrorists usually manage to find good speechwriters."

"I think not. I think that phrase is very important."

"What do you think it means?"

"I've no idea. But we better find out, before it's too late."

9

As the Stony Man team shifted into fighting gear, a search plane from Tinker Air Force Base, Oklahoma City, spotted the wreckage of the C-130.

The pilot caught the blackened path of the crash, then made a second pass at five hundred feet to pick up the markings on the tail.

"I've got it, Tinker." He gave the coordinates.

"Any sign of life?"

"Nothing," said the pilot. "Nobody walked away from that."

The fuselage had skidded several hundred yards up the low slope, shedding wings and odd bits and pieces. Fires had started when the fuel tanks exploded on impact, and the underbrush had burned from fifty to a hundred yards around the path of the slide. The fires had quickly burned themselves out for lack of ground fuel.

"All right, Search, thank you," came the voice from the ground. "We're already notifying the nearest civil authorities. They'll have ground teams in there before our own people arrive."

"They'll need all-terrain vehicles," the pilot said. "This country is badly broken up. No roads anywhere. They'll probably have to walk in the last three or four miles—I see a couple of gullies even an ATV won't be able to negotiate."

"Any indication of what caused the crash?"

"Not from up here, Tinker."

"All right, Search, well done. Come on home."

The search plane banked sharply and made a wide circle away from the wreckage, heading back to Oklahoma City. Tinker AFB was more than fifty minutes away at subsonic speed.

Several hours would pass before the first of the ground teams reached the C-130 and began the grisly task of digging out the bodies.

TWO HUNDRED MILES TO THE SOUTHWEST, a team of arson investigators from the state police picked a cautious way through the remains of the Collins house. They were aided by men from the local fire department, most of whom had been on the scene during the previous day's fire.

One man shouted to the others. "I found a couple!"

He studied the charred bodies as the professionals slogged over. "Jesus," he said, blanching. "These must be the kids."

"Here's another," said someone else, uncovering Hamilton Brownlow. The body was not recognizable.

Twenty minutes later Bobby and his mother were found together. "Hey," said one of the locals. "I thought there was only supposed to be four of them."

"Can't be the father," someone said. "They said he was on that plane they figured went down."

"Probably a friend," said a state man.

The bodies were loaded into meat wagons, to be delivered to the cold-storage room at the local hospital.

10

DAVID MCCARTER RECEIVED his first look at the legendary Emerald Isle. Perhaps because of his British reserve, he was unimpressed.

The Harrier jet, after landing at Belfast's Aldergrove air base, was met by a military-command car. As McCarter pulled his suitcase out of the cramped cockpit, a British major stepped out of the car.

"Laurence Dickman," said the major.

David took the proffered hand and was given a firm handshake.

"David McCarter."

Dickman held the door for McCarter, then settled heavily into his seat. "Quite a slap in the face for our friends across the water," he said. "I imagine the Americans aren't quite so pleased with the IRA boys today."

"IRA?" said David.

"They're all IRA in one form or another," said Dickman. "Call themselves Provos, Regulars, whatever; it's all cut from the same pudding. I must say, though, one must credit them for thinking so highly of themselves with this caper."

"Any update on the raids?"

"Nothing since we received word that you were on the way. Not that I understand exactly your position in this matter—just that I've been tapped as liaison. You'll really have to fill me in on what it is I'm supposed to do."

"At the moment your information is probably as up to date as mine," said David. "My first priority is for a secure link to my people on the other side."

"That we can do."

The command car motored on. The vehicle was heavily armored: steel shutters over the windows offered firing slits, and the windshield was triple-thick plate that would stop anything short of a rocket. McCarter peered through the slit and saw a shell-shocked city.

There were few men but many women on the street, and they turned away as the command car came into their block, showing their hatred for the men inside. Several women stopped and spit, and children threw stones that clanged against the armor.

A British soldier in full battle dress sat beside the driver, his rifle grounded between his feet. He hunched forward, staring through the windshield, the cords in his neck standing out with tension.

The street was potholed; the car jarred through the smaller, circled the biggest. Some holes were the result of mines that had destroyed other British vehicles, killed other British soldiers.

There were gaps in the buildings that lined the street; burned-out shells and lots filled with only rubble.

Dickman seemed relaxed, perhaps even bored, despite the tension of the youth in the front seat. The car stopped at a barricade manned by half a dozen soldiers with Bren guns. The major held up a laminated identity card, and the barrier was pulled aside. The car rolled through, into the heart of the city.

Civilian traffic was barred from downtown except for lorries making deliveries. Each van was checked thoroughly. There were more pedestrians, however, and for the first time the latter included a proportion of men from the surrounding offices and business establishments.

"We're going in bloody circles," McCarter said.

"Cook's tour," said Dickman. "Mandatory for every new arrival. Let's you see what the battle is all about."

"Who's got time for tours," McCarter growled, not causing too much fuss since he might need these guys later.

They left the broad thoroughfares and moved into a district of small streets that twisted and turned erratically. Rows of small, terraced houses lined the streets, although there was an occasional bombed-out shell. Small yards and alleyways abounded. In this district a thousand men could disappear, hide or set up ambush.

They passed from one religion's stronghold to the other. The streets and the houses looked the same and the hatred was back on the faces of the people. Belfast was a gray city under gray skies. It seemed no city for the good of spirit, those who meant well for their fellow men.

The command car came to a halt outside a walled building guarded by a concrete pillbox. Corrugated-iron sheets were angled against the wall, while the building was hung with camouflage net. Heavy mesh guarded the top of the walls and concertina wire filled the sidewalks.

"A police station," said Dickman dryly. "The mesh is to stop bombs from being thrown into the yard, and the corrugated sheets roll them back into the street."

Two men in riot gear opened the gate and the command car passed into the yard.

Inside, the building was more familiar, a typical cop shop, an aging structure that had seen better days. Green walls were flecked with peeling paint, and near the ceiling exposed pipes sweated. Men in the blue uniform of the Royal Ulster Constabulary moved through the corridors.

Dickman led McCarter to an office that had been furnished sixty years earlier. A heavy man in rumpled tweeds occupied a chair behind a desk. He stood and offered his hand as Dickman made the introductions.

"David McCarter, Inspector Donald MacMurray of the Royal Ulster Constabulary."

"Mr. McCarter," the inspector said. "I think we might have a line on your People's Republic of Ireland."

MacMurray sat and opened a folder. McCarter saw yellow sheets covered with handwriting.

"An informant phoned in this information not forty minutes ago," said the inspector. "He gave us a name: Seamus Riley."

"You know him?" McCarter asked.

"Riley's an old friend—a bold man, bold enough and crazy enough to come up with a scheme such as this. And uncaring enough to defy his fellows in the IRA by carrying the war to the United States."

He dug out a card from beneath the yellow sheets and gave it to David. It was a standard police identification card and showed Riley full face and in profile; he wore a numbered plaque around his neck. The card carried his fingerprints.

"Riley was an ISRA man," said MacMurray. "That's the Irish Socialist Republican Army, an offshoot of the Provos. Riley quarreled with the ISRA leadership and went his own way. He's done time—seven years for a bank robbery. He was released from prison eighteen months ago and dropped from sight. Rumor had it he was killed in a bombing, but Riley probably put that out about himself.''

"Do you know where he is?"

"Probably in the States," said MacMurray, "if he is masterminding this People's Republic thing. But Riley has a friend, Eamon O'Bannon. Boyhood chums, chased after each other's sister, the like. We can lay our hands on O'Bannon whenever we wish, and he might have some information."

"Where is he?"

"He spends his nights in a house near Crawfordsburn. That's about ten miles out toward Bangor. Between Holywood and Bangor. Days he's on the move, but he's been going back to that house every night for the past month."

"Then we'll take him tonight," said David.

THAT EVENING David huddled with MacMurray and Dickman in the back room of the Crawfordsburn RUC station, studying a map of the district. Dickman wanted to take the farmhouse in force, but David vetoed that idea. He had made a daylight probe of the area.

"He won't be alone," McCarter said. "Go in force and there'll be a firefight. We might lose him."

"How many others will be there?" asked Dickman.

"O'Bannon travels with half a dozen young lads," said MacMurray. "Sort of an honor guard. Whether there are others besides the guard depends on his business this day.''

"Give me thirty minutes," said David. "If I'm not out in that time come after me."

The backup force waited in Crawfordsburn. MacMurray warned against taking up position nearer the farm.

"Every house has its sympathizers. One man might slip through but any vehicle, even a bicycle, will be spotted."

McCarter jogged the distance in twenty minutes. The village near the farm had no more than thirty houses scattered along a mile or more of narrow, turning lane. The only house that showed a light was the pub.

Twice dogs barked, and less than a mile away traffic moved on the A2. Using the information gained in his drive through the village that afternoon, and by studying the map, McCarter jogged across a field, halving the distance it would have taken him had he traveled by road.

The farmyard was a different place at night; shadows cast by the light of the moon produced a maze of strange shapes and looming traps. A line of darker shadow covered a hole deep enough to catch a foot, twist an ankle. The half-collapsed barn was a crouching beast, menacing the unwary.

McCarter slipped behind a tree as soon as he reached the farm and stood there for several minutes, probing the night with his senses. Trying to spot the presence of a sentry. The house was absolutely dark. If not for MacMurray's assurances, he would have passed it by for what it seemed to be: abandoned.

Then McCarter heard the metallic clack of a gun bolt behind him. Bleeding bastard must have been hiding in the goddamn bushes, he thought as he whirled to face a young terrorist who was armed with a Swedish M-45 machine gun.

The Briton's combat-honed reflexes had already commanded his muscles to draw the Colt Python from shoulder leather. Years of pistol shooting took over as he snap-aimed and fired before the kid could use his weapon. A scream escaped from the terrorist when the Colt belched fire and a 158-grain wadcutter blasted through the boy's chest. The young rebel was pitched backward by the impact of the slug. His finger pulled the M-45's trigger as he fell, rattling off a chain of bullets into the sky.

"Bloody hell," McCarter growled. More terrorists suddenly materialized in all directions.

He hit the dirt as a stream of 7.62mm projectiles hissed overhead. McCarter held the Colt in a two-handed Weaver's grip and fired from a prone position, aiming at the muzzle flash of the enemy's AK-47. A scream rewarded his efforts and one of the shadows fell.

A figure suddenly charged toward McCarter from the side. David rolled on his back, swinging the Colt around...too late. A boot lashed out and kicked the Briton's hand, ripping the

Colt from numbed fingers. The terrorist raised an assault rifle and brought the butt stock down, trying to slam it through McCarter's face.

David jerked his head aside, and the rifle butt stamped into the ground near his ear. McCarter's legs thrust upward, both feet kicking his opponent in the gut. The terrorist gasped and staggered backward while McCarter scrambled to his feet.

"Goddamn sod!" the terrorist snarled as he swung a vicious butt stroke at McCarter's head.

The Englishman ducked from the rifle's path. Metal and wood whistled overhead. McCarter lunged, driving a shoulder into the startled terrorist's midsection. Then he seized the fellow's legs and standing up, scooped up his adversary and hurled him over his head. The man crashed to the ground hard. McCarter immediately executed a "commando stomp," smashing the heels of both boots into the terrorist's chest. The man's breastbone exploded, driving fragments into his heart and lungs.

McCarter reached for the rifle while the rebel's body convulsed beneath his feet. More Irish killers swarmed over McCarter before he could grab the weapon. A fist holding a revolver swung at his head. McCarter blocked it with a forearm and drove his other fist into the attacker's stomach, followed by a left hook to the Irishman's face.

The man fell, but another took his place. Mc-

Carter dodged a slashing rifle barrel and kicked his adversary in the gut. The terrorist grunted, doubled up and the edge of McCarter's hand chopped into the back of his neck.

Then something crashed into McCarter's skull from behind. Pain exploded inside his head for an instant, only to be swallowed up by the blackness that quickly engulfed McCarter's consciousness.

"Why didn't you shoot him, Eamon?" asked a young rebel as McCarter slumped to the ground.

"Where there is one Brit, lad, there are others, and likely close at hand. I want this one, if he lives, to talk. He didn't come alone. Go to the house and wake the other lads, tell them to clear out. We'll meet at the church."

Twenty minutes later, Dickman led a squad of soldiers and RUCs into the farmyard. Lights blazed and orders were barked loudly as they moved into the house and searched the barn.

The house was empty, one kerosene lamp burning. The barn contained two cars, which had been stolen in London. There was nothing else to suggest the terrorists had ever been there.

11

SOMEONE, SOMETHING, was turning a screw that tightened the metal band that had been fastened around David McCarter's head. His head throbbed in rhythm with each pulse of his heart, the blood vessels expanding, until it seemed that only his skull kept them from exploding.

In agony, McCarter awoke. A brass drum sounded loudly in his head. He choked, holding back any audible sound of pain. A sickly taste had taken over his mouth. He tried to raise a hand to touch his head, but his arm refused to obey.

He tried to move, but his hands were bound behind his back. His ankles were also tied.

He lay on his left side, facing a wall of cracked, splintering, unpainted boards. McCarter closed his eyes, taking inventory of his aches and pains. Except for his skull, none seemed life threatening.

His hands were cold from loss of circulation. Also, the place—room, barn, whatever it was— was damp, chilly. Somewhere behind him was a heat source that pulsed erratically. He breathed

and caught the carbon stink of burning kerosene.

Someone moved, shifting position. Dry wood
creaked.

Someone else snorted in sleep, turned over,
and began to snore.

McCarter was not alone.

He listened and caught two, three distinct
rhythms of breathing sleepers. The smell of the
smoke was sickening. His stomach rumbled in
anger. It was empty.

When had he last eaten?

McCarter searched his memory, ignoring his
aches and pains. He recalled a hurried supper
with Dickman and MacMurray, in the Belfast
police station.

The condition of his stomach said that more
than twelve hours had passed, perhaps much
more. That made it the following day, although
no glimmer of daylight entered this room. The
room was closed tightly; from the dampness, it
might be underground. A cave?

Perhaps a full twenty-four hours had passed,
making it evening again.

What happened after the supper? The plan
was to wait until midnight, give the nearby
village a chance to settle for the night, but Mc-
Carter's memories were blank after the meal.

McCarter considered rolling over. He lay on a
bare mattress that stank of mildew. A button
dug into his cheek.

A door closed, causing air currents to ripple

across the room. Heavy footsteps came downstairs. Someone breathed noisily through an
open mouth. Wood creaked again as one of the
guards in the room got up from his chair.

"Is he awake yet?"

"He hasn't moved, Eamon." The voice was
high and clear. "Once I thought he stopped
breathing. He hadn't."

Eamon. Eamon O'Bannon.

"Let's take a look at him," said O'Bannon.

They crossed the floor and the noisy breathing came closer. A hand caught McCarter's
shoulder and rolled him onto his back. The
position was even more uncomfortable because
of his bound hands. McCarter could not contain
a groan. He arched his back to ease the pressure
on his wrists.

"You're awake, Brit. Good."

McCarter blinked, and O'Bannon's face
came into focus, bending over him. His lips
parted widely. He worked his jaws in a gulping
motion, scraped his coated tongue against his
teeth.

The man turned to the boy who stood at nis
shoulder. "Water, Paulie. We'll see if he has
anything to tell us."

The water was brackish, metallic to the taste,
but it soaked into the tissues and eased Mc-
Carter's sore throat. He gulped, swallowing
greedily, as O'Bannon held the cup. Liquid
slopped out, running down his cheeks and neck.

"You might be surprised to find you're still

alive, Brit,'' said O'Bannon, giving the cup back to Paulie, who was a mere boy of seventeen. ''That's a condition that can be changed very quickly, McCarter.''

''Sorry, I don't remember making introductions,'' McCarter commented, wincing as pain stabbed across his skull.

''I'm Eamon O'Bannon,'' the Irishman replied. ''And I know who you are 'cause I found your dogtags. Fitting that the British give their soldiers dogtags, 'cause you're all sons of bitches.''

''That's pretty good,'' McCarter snorted. ''Did you hear about the retarded Scot? They sent him to Ireland to teach college courses. . . .''

O'Bannon's big arm streaked out, the back of his hand slapping McCarter across the mouth. The Englishman's already pounding head recoiled from the blow, and blood trickled from a split lip.

''You've killed three of my boys, Brit!'' O'Bannon bellowed. ''That's reason enough for us to pull you apart like a bloody insect, so mind your tongue unless you want me to cut it off and stick it . . . .''

''I didn't come here to kill anyone,'' McCarter said thickly. ''I had to defend myself. Your men didn't leave me any choice. I'm trying to avoid killing.''

''That's why you had a gun, eh?'' O'Bannon sneered.

David glanced around. He was in a cellar, exposed beams in the ceiling not more than an inch or so above normal head height. O'Bannon had to duck to get under them. Two broad tree trunks, two or more feet thick, supported the ceiling.

Two of the walls were boards, the others rough-dressed stone. The floor was dirt. There were shelves against the board walls, similar to the one on which he lay, and a half-dozen iron cots. Three of the cots were occupied. The heat came from a portable kerosene stove, the light from a kerosene lamp on a battered wood kitchen table. The light did not reach the corners, which were shadowed and menacing with indistinct piles of boxes and jumbled furniture. A wooden church pew was on one side of the table, several battered kitchen chairs on the other.

The table held two Bren guns, an Uzi and two Kalashnikovs. An open wooden crate on the floor carried military stenciling and held grenades. The boy had a machine pistol slung from one shoulder, which he held on McCarter.

"We're not at the farm?" McCarter asked.

"Never mind where we are, Brit," O'Bannon told him. "Now, what were you sneakin' around us for? What were you after?"

"I have to find Seamus Riley."

"Oh? You plan to join the People's Republic, Brit?" O'Bannon smiled thinly.

"He has to be stopped, O'Bannon," McCarter replied. "If he succeeds in carrying this war to the United States, *everybody* will suffer...including Ireland and all you noble revolutionaries who fight for God, glory and cheap whiskey."

O'Bannon rammed a big fist into McCarter's stomach. McCarter gasped as the blow drove the wind from his lungs. "I told you about that big mouth of yours, Brit," the Irishman said. "As for stopping Seamus, I'm afraid you're a bit too late for that."

McCarter drew fresh air into his lungs before he spoke. "What do you mean by that?"

"Seamus has been busy...if he is, as they say, the lad behind the People's Republic."

"You don't know?"

"It has Seamus's stamp. Mind you, it's not that we, the forces of Irish liberation, agree with what he's doing. But Seamus has given us a fait accompli, don't you know. It's not do we agree, but do we stand with him or against him. There's been a council meeting, the first I can remember, where every party in the fight has been represented."

"Both sides?" said David.

"Hardly. It's not a matter to discuss with the Prots."

"Have they reached a decision?"

"They're comin' to it. Seamus hasn't given us much time. We'll have to make our stand before this night is done. I've given my vote, and were I a betting man I'd say the decision would be to stand with him."

"You're all daft," McCarter muttered with disgust. "A goddamned madman is going to carry out an insane plan, which you don't even know the details of, and you're agreeing to it because of some peanut-brained idea of unity!"

"If I were you, I'd be more concerned about yourself McCarter," O'Bannon stated in a cold, hard voice.

"Why?" challenged the Englishman, glaring at his captor. "You're going to kill me anyway, so go piss up a rope, O'Bannon."

"Aye." The Irishman nodded. "After killing three of my lads, your life isn't worth a wooden shilling. How you'll die is the question, Brit. We can make it quick with a bullet in your head, or slow. Very slow, McCarter. Maybe we'll use a drill on your kneecaps and elbows then pour hot tar down your throat. How's that sound?"

"Don't expect me to die of heart failure from listening to your horror stories," McCarter scoffed. "You do your damnedest, but don't expect me to crawl for you, you great dirty ape."

"Oh, you'll crawl, McCarter," O'Bannon said with a smile. "You'll crawl on your ruddy knees and beg us to kill you before...."

An explosion sounded overhead, the distant crump of a grenade. It was followed by two more muffled crashes and then by automatic-weapons fire, a sound as welcome as music to McCarter's ears.

O'Bannon spun as bodies tumbled from the cots and rushed for the weapons on the table. A youth came rushing down the stairs, shouting a warning.

"The church is surrounded, Eamon!"

"How many?" cried O'Bannon.

"I don't know, but they're on all sides. We're outnumbered. They've left us no way out!"

Then McCarter heard return fire, louder, overhead. From the volume, there were many defenders above.

A large crump sounded directly overhead; dirt rattled from the beams and the floorboards and rained down on McCarter. Another mortar round landed. McCarter rolled, throwing himself onto the floor as a hole opened above him. The ancient planks of the floor were split in two.

Another youth came running down the stairs. "Eamon, the church is afire!"

"Upstairs, lads!" said O'Bannon. "Move! We haven't a chance if we stay here!"

They rushed the stairs and disappeared. The sound of small arms joined the hellish concert. Fire licked the edges of the hole. The cellar was warming rapidly. The kerosene stove had been knocked over, spilling liquid flames onto the dirt floor. They licked at the table, caught hold and sent a fire finger up the leg, blistering the paint. The puddle of burning kerosene reached the corner of the box of grenades.

McCarter lay on his face. The dirt of the floor felt deathly cold against his cheek. He wormed his way forward. Working his knees under his belly, he managed to push himself up to a kneeling position. He settled back on his heels.

The centuries-old wood of the church burned like tinder. Already the fire roared above. Flames ate their way through the cracks between the floorboards of the church, licked at them from underneath and joined together.

McCarter listened to the battle, knowing he was trapped. He had no way out.

12

LATE-APRIL SUNSHINE threatened the San Fernando Valley with the heat of midsummer. From Reseda Boulevard eastward the smog settled in early, filling the eyes and choking the lungs of the people who lived in Van Nuys and Studio City, Panorama City and Glendale. The area became engulfed by a yellow green haze of smog. By noon, the Air Quality Management District Board called a first-stage smog alert for the first time that season.

In Burbank, a delivery van wheeled out of an alley behind a block of stores, weaving erratically as it bumped into San Fernando Boulevard and turned south. Brakes squealed in anger as the van cut off a car. A Harley hog sliced out of traffic and roared around the van, the biker glancing sideways to give the driver the finger. He blinked.

"Sweet Jesus!"

The bike swerved as the rider took a second look then quickly fed gas to the bike. He cut off two cars and reclaimed a lane in the crowded street. He then checked the mirrors on his handlebars. The van was three cars back, the windshield blank.

There was no driver! The van was being operated by remote control. And at the control was a lunatic who worked for another lunatic, Seamus Riley.

The van continued its trek. It motored along, reaching a block that contained an eight-story parking garage and, beside it, a twelve-story office building. A pedestrian bridge crossed from the sixth story of the garage to the office building. On the north side of the building, was a branch office of the Colonial-Far Eastern Bank of California.

The van, running the crazed course it was given, veered abruptly and bumped over the curb, nearly hitting a man standing at a bus stop. The van sped across the plaza, through flower beds and scattering pedestrians.

People shouted. People ran for their lives. A woman screamed, snatching a small child out of the way. The van crushed the corner of a temporary plywood bandstand, set up for lunchtime concerts. The van then stopped with its bumper against the front door of the bank.

A woman had just pushed the door open to leave. The collision with the van knocked her back into the lobby. She gathered air into her lungs to protest but had no time to exhale as a ton of dynamite in the van exploded with an ear-shattering bang.

The fireball filled the area, melting the shards

of plate-glass that still hung in their storefront frames, scorching everything within the shops and turning it to lumps of carbon.

In the bank's lobby, the explosion shredded ceiling tiles and tore carpeting away from the concrete subfloor in strips that flared like candlewicks. The tellers' counter slammed back against the wall, trapping a dozen dead bodies. The half-dozen desks used by the manager, assistant manager, loans officers and the new-accounts clerk were blown against the back wall. And so were the bodies of the men and women who manned those desks.

Every window in the three blocks facing San Fernando Boulevard was blown out, glass falling into the streets. There was instant madness as drivers tried to react; cars in front of the office building were thrown across the street by the force of the blast, while the next ten seconds saw dozens of collisions between cars driven by panicked drivers. Windows were cracked in the loading-gate area at Hollywood-Burbank Airport, half a mile away, and in more than a thousand other buildings. The blast's muscle flex was felt in Glendale and in Sunland, in Hollywood and North Hollywood, across half the Valley.

Some thought it was the beginning of World War III. Others thought it was an earthquake. All felt the terror of the blast.

The rolling fireball scoured the plaza, killing every pedestrian on the block. The pedestrian bridge to the garage cracked, shifting nearly six inches. The concrete side of the garage was scorched black, a blackness that spread as it rose.

Other persons, blocks away, were knocked flat, or even thrown into the street—some dying under squealing tires. The fireball was the only visible force of destruction, but the blast carved a six-foot-deep crater out of the ground. The van, except for odd bits and pieces, had vaporized.

Two survivors were found on the fifth floor, a few more on the sixth and many more on the other six floors of the building. But even the twelfth floor had its casualties: people crushed beneath tumbling bookcases and collapsing ceilings, trapped behind desks thrown against walls. Others, bleeding and in shock, died waiting for rescue. A descending elevator was blown apart at the seventh floor.

The Army of the People's Republic of Ireland had struck, and in spectacular fashion.

They had not waited seventy-two hours.

KEIO OHARA stood on a pedestrian overpass, watching the frantic scene below.

Sirens screamed in the distance. Fire trucks and ambulances hooted, the clamor of the air horns rising in register as they raced nearer.

A blue-and-white police helicopter chattered noisily overhead, airfoil kicking up dust and garbage. The wind tore at Keio's hair and he squinted against the dust devils.

A dozen highway-patrol cars blocked the six lanes of the freeway, stopping dead the usual heavy L.A. midday traffic. The bottleneck reached back into the Hollywood Hills, a mile away, and congestion was heavy on the intersecting Pasadena and Glendale freeways. Occupants of the vehicles leaned through windows or stood in the narrow lanes between cars, staring at the disaster.

Beyond the barricade of cruisers, the freeway was empty except for cars and victims involved in a dozen accidents, and three fire trucks that had made it onto the roadway by entering via the next exit ramp. The fire trucks pumped streams of water into the office tower above, where black columns of smoke billowed into the sky.

Keio had arrived on the scene twenty minutes earlier, pausing only for a hasty conference with the Burbank deputy police chief who had taken charge of the command post that had been set up in a secondhand bookstore. The previous night, after receiving instructions from Stony Man, Keio had come to Los Angeles to coordinate local search efforts. The chopper overhead had brought him from L.A. police headquarters.

Emotions seething, he watched the scene. He felt a hatred so powerful he knew it could not be contained.

Scores, perhaps hundreds, of lives lost.

A twelve-million-dollar building destroyed.

The building was owned by the bank, which used it as its regional headquarters, but there were six floors of other tenants, fifty or sixty other companies in no way connected to Great Britain; companies whose only crime was to be on the scene, in a war zone.

Insanity.

Madness.

A cop got out of a patrol car and called out: "Ohara!"

Keio took a last look at the freeway and ran to the car. He accepted the microphone and thumbed the talk switch.

"Ohara."

The radio crackled noisily, making the dispatcher's voice hard to understand. Keio listened carefully then looked at the cop.

"How close is El Toro Marine Air Station?"

"That's down in Orange County. Sixty or seventy miles."

Keio glanced at the circling chopper. It had dropped him on a residential street on the far side of the freeway, and now waited to carry him wherever he wanted to go. He relayed his instructions through the dispatcher, returned the microphone to the cop, then started to run across the walkway. Before he reached the other side, the chopper veered off, heading for the landing place.

"El Toro Air Station," Keio yelled to the pilot as he hopped into the bird's belly.

"Right!" said the pilot, shouting to be heard over the racket of the airfoil. "We're on our way!"

Keio put on headphones and the noise was cut to an almost bearable level. As the chopper passed over the city of Los Angeles, he listened to the police band. Most of the reports were about the bombing. Thus far, one hundred thirty bodies had been removed from the streets surrounding the office tower and from neighboring buildings.

Keio stared down at the unrolling city—sixty small towns in search of an identity. Thirty minutes later the housing developments ended, and they were over the open land of El Toro Marine Air Station. Another five minutes and he was on the ground, climbing into the cockpit of a Harrier VTOL jet.

As he boarded, the pilot gave him thumbs-up and Keio settled his six-foot frame in the cramped cockpit. He was traveling without luggage and without weapons, except for his own lethal hands and feet. Trained in kendo and judo, holder of a black belt in karate and student of all martial arts, Keio was a human time bomb. Walking into a confrontation never worried him. He could take care of himself.

The pilot reached Stony Man Farm and set the jet fighter down within the circle marked on the helicopter pad.

Rafael Encizo was on his way by jet to Stony Man from Kelly Air Force Base, San Antonio. When Rafael reached Stony Man Farm he was hit with the news: the truth of the crash of the C-130 had been discovered.

"The balloon just went up," Yakov told Rafael. "We know what the terrorists meant when they called themselves the fury bomb. *They're nuclear.*"

Rafael uttered a prayer that was equally a curse, and crossed himself.

"Also, David's been taken."

Madre de Dios! "What do we do?" he asked.

"We take him back."

13

THE LEADERS of the Army of the People's Republic of Ireland had gathered in the living room of an abandoned farmhouse in Chenango County, New York. The owner had gone broke because of high interest rates and runaway inflation. Three of the four nearest farms were no longer operational.

Seamus Riley had rented the house as a base for his Irish insanity.

Riley, Liam Clune and three other men watched the evening news on a 13-inch color TV. Story after story reported about the California bombing.

"In a bulletin just handed me," a stone-faced newsreader intoned, "it says the death toll in the Burbank bombing has risen to one hundred eighty. It is a major tragedy. The nation is in shock, our people in mourning."

Commercials rolled on. Riley smiled at the brutal effectiveness of the news. But none of the five men spoke, still waiting for the announcement of whether their demands would be met. The last commercial dissolved, and the TV anchorman returned.

"In New York today, a spokesman for the fifty companies chosen as targets of the terrorists' extortion demands announced that follow-up letters have been received, repeating the original demands."

The station switched to a news conference. Cameras zoomed in on a forty-year-old man in a rumpled suit standing before a battery of microphones that bore the logos of major television and radio stations. Heads bobbed as photographers jostled to gain vantage points. Several reporters shouted out questions.

"Mr. Lowell!" a reporter fired at the beleaguered spokesman, "are the companies going to pay?"

"Absolutely not! Representatives of the companies have been meeting since yesterday. It had already been agreed that no payments would be made. The companies remain united in their decision—they will not give in to extortion."

"The idiots!" Seamus Riley slammed a fist against the arm of his overstuffed chair. "The bloody fools!"

"Seamus," Liam said. "Listen, he's sayin' more."

The spokesman held up his hand, trying to still the rattle of the reporters. At last they quieted enough for his words to come through.

"Ladies and gentlemen, please! Please. Thank you." He gripped the edges of the podium.

"I have been authorized to announce that the

companies involved are offering a reward of one million dollars for the capture of the leaders responsible for these outrages!''

Bedlam again; the picture jumped, showing the ceiling of the room for an instant as someone jostled the cameraman.

The station returned to the newsman in the studio.

''The offer of a one-million-dollar reward for the capture of the leaders of the terrorist group calling itself the Army of the People's Republic of Ireland is most unusual. The normal offering of such a reward stipulates that it will be paid upon the arrest and conviction of the perpetrators of a crime. We now return you to the news conference for an update.''

A haggard looking roving reporter came on camera. ''We do have further details of the reward offer,'' she said. ''As you heard earlier, the companies have banded together to offer one million dollars for the capture of the leaders of the Army of the People's Republic of Ireland, but that is inaccurate, the reward is just for the leaders. It is estimated that between one hundred fifty and two hundred men took part in the raids, and there is a further reward of ten thousand dollars for the arrest and conviction of any of those men. However, let me repeat, the million-dollar offer is for the capture of the leaders.''

The station then cut to a ''promo,'' promising sports and entertainment news had not been forgotten in the chaos over the attacks.

"Turn if off!"

The leader glowered at the screen while the picture shrunk into a dot and faded. None of the other four dared break the silence.

"The fools." Riley's voice was flat, dead. "I warned them. I gave them a chance."

"What do we do now, Seamus?" Liam asked.

"Perhaps we should call it off," said another.

"Call it off?" said Riley. "It's a bold soldier of freedom you are, Cavan Coakley."

"They won't pay, Seamus," said a young terrorist. "We'll not see a penny."

"If the Brit companies won't pay, Doyle MacGrew, we will collect from someone else."

"Who, Seamus?" said Liam, not hiding his worry.

"The Americans, Liam."

The others said nothing, but the turmoil in their thoughts showed on their faces. Liam Clune could see that none of them liked it. But even he dared not speak in opposition, for fear of the violent nature of the man beside him.

"We have the bomb," said Riley. "We'll give the Americans one chance to see that when Seamus Riley speaks, he means what he says. One chance, and this time they will listen."

He pulled himself from the chair, stood there staring at the dead television.

"But the price has gone up," said Riley. "Liam, the photographs taken when the warheads were removed from the missiles, I want them. And Cavan, a new letter, this time to the President of the United States and the leaders of Congress. Send copies to the television networks, AP, UPI and the major newspapers—*The New York Times*, the *Washington Post*, the *Los Angeles Times*, the lot of them.''

"And what do we say this time, Seamus?'' Coakley asked.

"We say that we have four atomic bombs. The photographs will be proof of that. Unless the money transfer goes through as ordered, one bomb will be exploded in the heart of a major city. Give them forty-eight hours. And another bomb each forty-eight hours thereafter, until they come to their senses and do as we say.''

"How much are we asking?'' said Coakley.

"A good sum,'' said Riley. He smiled. "A round sum. One they will easily remember. One billion dollars.''

14

RAFAEL ENCIZO AND KEIO OHARA met at Stony
Man Farm. The two Phoenix Force agents
clasped arms briefly; they had become good
friends during their fights against the forces of
terrorism. They were in the War Room with
Yakov.

April Rose appeared, an attractive one-
woman welcoming party, carrying a tray that
held coffee for Rafael, a cup of Japanese green
tea for Keio.

"We may have a line on David," said Yakov.
"Things are breaking for us. The IRA factions
have sent an offer of help—they took a vote and
most decided they resented Riley's taking the
war to America."

"Nothing yet on the terrorists in the raids?"
asked Keio.

"Nothing," said Yakov. "It's incredible, but
a hundred fifty men have vanished from the
face of the earth."

"They had safehouses ready," Rafael said.
"They're smart enough to stay buried—this
man Riley is smart enough to keep them
buried."

"We're still working on that aspect," said Yakov, "but for now it's in the hands of the police. They're far more capable in such matters. They can mount a search with hundreds, if necessary, thousands of men. Gary is in Sussex looking for Riley and the stolen warheads."

Keio raised an eyebrow; he had not been briefed on the latter. Katzenelenbogen filled him in quickly and he nodded.

"They are truly crazed and very dangerous. Nuclear weapons do them no good unless they are willing to use them."

"This Riley bastard may be just that crazy," said Rafael.

"I hate to split our forces," said Yakov, "but we don't seem to have much choice at the moment. You two are going to Ireland to find David—Brognola has an Air Force fighter jet ready for the flight."

Rafael glanced at a table, covered with weapons: two Ingrams; an Uzi; side arms that included John Phoenix's preferred Beretta and Rafael's own favorite gun, the 7.65mm Vzor 61, the Czech Skorpion. There was also a grenade launcher, Startron night sights by Smith & Wesson and ammunition for everything. The weapons that could be broken down for transport had been. The others waited storage in two field packs that lay open on another table.

"We don't know what you'll be facing,"

said Yakov. "Be ready for anything. Your liaison in Belfast is a Major Dickman of the British army and Inspector MacMurray of the Royal Ulster Constabulary."

Rafael nodded, then he and Keio moved to the table to prepare the packs.

"I want to go with you," Yakov said, "but things may break here at any time. If the two of you can't break David free...."

He left the sentence hanging. The two men turned and departed.

The Harrier was gone when they reached the helicopter pad. One of the black-painted choppers had taken its place. The airfoil had already begun to turn as they ran across the grass and plunged through the door. Rafael scrambled to take the seat near the pilot. Keio remained in the rear with the field packs. Both put on earphones.

The chopper took them directly to an airfield and set them down within twenty yards of an Air Force jet.

The pair boarded the plane. Once in the air, Keio drew an Ingram Model 10 from his pack. The telescopic stock was closed. In that mode, the length of the gun was 10.6 inches, the barrel 5¾ inches. He screwed a noise suppressor onto the muzzle, adding another 10.85 inches to the length. The Ingram was chambered for 9mm cartridges. Keio added a 32-round box magazine. Ready for action after Keio worked the slide, the Ingram now weighed about nine pounds. In automatic mode, the Ingram fired ninety-six rounds per minute; single shot, forty rounds per minute. The maximum effective range was one hundred eight yards.

Keio worked quietly, intent on disassembling the Ingram, satisfied it was in functioning order. No weapon left Stony Man's armory in anything but top functioning order. In a pinch, he could have gone straight into battle without double-checking. Keio, however, needed something to occupy his mind during the flight.

Rafael finished checking his weapons and settled back, folding his hands across his stomach and closing his eyes. He had his own method for seeking additional strength and killing time. He slept.

THE CITY SPARKLED like a jewel in the early-evening darkness as the plane dropped its nose and then its tail, settling toward the runway.

Once Belfast's sparkle had come from its inhabitants, but those people had lost much of their luster in the continuing fighting.

Belfast, the capital of Northern Ireland and the center of the British province's strife, has lost more than twenty-five percent of its population since 1971. Once standing at a proud 416,679, the population has plummeted to 297,983. The wars in this world have taken their toll.

Phoenix Force fighters were entering the Irish war zone. David McCarter's life was at stake.

The jet landed.

They were met by Major Dickman and his command car. The British officer offered his hand.

"Any trace of McCarter?" Keio asked.

"We've got a meeting with an informant at a pub in twenty minutes," said Dickman. "Actually, all hell's breaking loose. I've never seen the like—IRA men openly consorting with the police and the military. They're more than peeved with this maniac, Riley."

"The IRA draws much of its financial support from Irish Americans," said Rafael.

"Not as much as people might suppose," said Dickman. "A lot of the lolly comes from North Africa. But they certainly count on the goodwill of the Americans. This has caused a good lot of people to get rightly pissed off."

The car made its way to the pub.

The field packs were left in the command car, although both Keio and Rafael were armed with knives and ankle guns. Major Dickman glanced about nervously before he opened the door and entered the pub.

There were only a few men in the public bar, and they were caught between staring at Dickman with undisguised hatred and looking with astonishment at the presence of a Japanese and a Cuban. Dickman gave notice of their presence by ignoring them and pushed through into the private bar, which had been taken over by Inspector MacMurray for this meeting.

MacMurray sat with a ferret-faced little man, nursing a pint of bitters. He did not bother to rise for the Phoenix Force agents but nodded amiably when Dickman made the introductions.

"A brew before business, gentlemen?" He raised his pint.

"Another time," said Keio. "Is this the man who knows where David is being held?"

"Girvin Kearney," MacMurray said. "As black a scoundrel as ever stole the washing off a poor woman's clothesline. He should be in Long Kesh for consorting and aiding the rebels, but God's luck has been with Girvin, it has."

"He should be standing before a firing squad," said Dickman, making no effort to conceal his distaste for the little man. Kearney pulled back sharply in his chair.

"Here, now! No recriminations, you said, Inspector."

"And I'm a man of my word, Kearney. You said you have a message. Out with it."

"I do, from Cormick Heffernan himself. And its Heffernan who sent me here, Inspector."

"Heffernan is a top man with the Provos," said MacMurray to Rafael and Keio. "Well, Girvin?"

"Eamon O'Bannon is your man."

"We know that!" said Dickman in disgust. "Where is he holding him, you bloody fool?"

"In St. Bridget's Church," said Kearney sourly.

"Which St. Bridget's?" said MacMurray. "The one this side of Londonderry?"

"No, the abandoned one on the south shore of Lough Foyle. Between Limavady and Ballykelly. O'Bannon's had it for a safehouse and a weapons depot. He's there now with his lads and perhaps a half dozen more."

"And?" prompted MacMurray. "Give us the rest of it, or I'll let the major run you into Long Kesh for a proper interrogation."

Kearney winced and drew a slip of paper from a pocket. He placed it on the table and pushed it to the exact center, eyeing it unhappily.

Dickman picked it up. "Neal Riordan, 14 Great Jones Street. In London?"

"No, in New York," said Kearney. "Riordan is married to O'Bannon's sister, but before she emigrated she was Riley's girl. Riordan set it up for Riley and his boys to slip into the States from Canada. Riley himself went across at East Franklin, Vermont."

"And Riordan knows where Riley is now," said MacMurray.

"It stands to reason, doesn't it?" said Kearney bitterly. He did not enjoy the role of informant.

"Well done," said MacMurray, standing.

"We'll transmit this information to the proper authorities. You can take my thanks back to Cormick Heffernan. Tell himself it's a good thing he does for the IRA today."

The other three rose and followed him from the pub. As they came out into the street, the command car rounded the corner.

"Do you think he was telling the truth?" said Dickman.

"Cormick Heffernan has no reason to lie in this case," said MacMurray. "He's been bitter since Riley walked away from the Provos, and that was ten years ago. I believe him."

"And we'll act as though we believe him," said Rafael. "How long will it take us to reach St. Bridget's Church?"

"It's a good hundred kilometers by road," said MacMurray. "It would be quicker to fly to Londonderry and drive back on the A2."

"We'll need time to ready a team on that end," said Dickman. "Call out a troop from the Londonderry barracks. They should be ready by the time you reach there."

"No," said Rafael. He glanced at Keio. "Do you agree, *compadre*? No soldiers."

Keio nodded. "We will go in alone."

"That's ridiculous!" said MacMurray. "Kearney said there are a dozen men with O'Bannon."

"We go in alone," said Rafael. "That's the way we work."

MacMurray shook his head. The two bloody

fools could go in by themselves, but he would have a backup team ready to go in when O'Bannon and his men shot them down.

He did not know Phoenix Force.

15

THE CHURCH OF ST. BRIDGET stood atop a broad hill overlooking Lough Foyle, the largest inlet in the north coast of Ireland. Fed by the River Foyle, the lough at its south shore was eleven miles wide and extended just over twenty miles until it narrowed to a mouth only three-quarters of a mile wide, between Inishowen Head and Magilligan Point. After studying maps, Keio and Rafael agreed that land approaches would be the most closely watched.

"We'll go in by water," said Rafael.

Three hours after landing at Aldergrove, a small lorry pulled off the A2 two miles west of St. Bridget's and picked its way through an overgrown lane that was scarcely two ruts in the field. It stopped at last on the rocky beach. Keio and Rafael waited in back, dressed in combat suits that made them part of the night. The moon hung low to the west, frequently obscured by clouds. Within fifteen minutes it would drop behind Mount Scalp.

A cold wind blew steadily from the lough as the two Phoenix Force agents pulled an inflatable raft from the lorry and dragged it to the edge of the water. Rafael went back for the mortar, the one piece of armament borrowed from the locals. They had sorted through the weapons supplied by Stony Man, choosing what they would need for the hit. Each agent now carried an Ingram, a Beretta in a belt holster and a Mark IV knife. Rafael also had his Skorpion, refusing to part with it. Each had a dozen grenades clipped to the front of his suit, and Rafael carried a half-dozen mortar rounds in an open-work carrier of steel wire.

They pushed the raft into the lough, walked through several inches of bone-chilling water and got in. Keio took up the oars. By the time he had rowed twenty yards out, the lorry was a shadowed lump in the midst of the waist-high gorse.

Neither spoke. Keio's labored breathing and the tiny splash of the oars were the only sounds to disturb the silence of the night. Rafael fingered the Skorpion; the Ingram was slung across his back.

The lough was deserted and empty of houses on this stretch of beach. Keio's muscles worked heavily as he moved the raft at a speed that quickly brought them closer to their target. After twenty minutes, Rafael raised a hand and Keio stopped rowing.

"There, on the hill," said Rafael softly. His voice was no louder than a whisper and reached no farther than his partner.

Keio nodded. The hill and the church were

about five hundred yards away. The building, abandoned for a hundred years or more, might have been no more than part of the irregular shape of the hill itself. No light showed, but they knew men were there.

Keio lifted one oar from the water and used the other to angle the boat toward the shore. In less than a minute, they were ankle deep in the lough again. They quickly pulled the raft across the beach and turned it upside down at the edge of the gorse. The two agents settled on their heels, studying the church.

A light flared: a match touched to a cigarette. The ember glowed brighter as the terrorist drew the first suck of smoke deep into his lungs, then faded slightly. Keio touched Rafael's arm. The Cuban nodded, to show he had seen the sentry.

Keio shrugged the Ingram from his shoulder and gave it to Rafael. He then drew a wire garrote from his sleeve. Short wood handles on either end gave his hands something to grip. He tested the wire, pulling the weapon out wide as the sentry came down a path to the shore. He then moved forward in a low crouch, looking like a shadow cast by a cloud.

The sentry paused on the beach, staring out across the lough. He drew a last drag from the cigarette and flicked it into the water. He then heard a pebble rattle and started to turn, Kalashnikov still slung on his shoulder.

He was too late. The garrote wire snapped tight around his neck, and with a single surge of strength Keio stripped his breath before the sentry could rattle a warning. The victim's back arched and he kicked out. His hands came up to his throat as he tried to reach back and claw at the enemy who had come from the night, but the knee in the small of his back held him too far away to be effective.

The struggle lessened, subsided to feet kicking feebly at the pebbles. The body then slumped in death. Keio released him and coiled the wire around his upper left arm. A twist of the handles locked it in place; another would free it again just as quickly. He moved back to Rafael.

Keio retrieved his Ingram, and they advanced another hundred yards down the beach. A narrow path wound through the gorse, circling the knoll.

Rafael touched Keio's arm and moved up the path with mortar in one hand, mortar rounds in the other. Keio checked his watch. Rafael would fire the first round in five minutes. He had that much time to get to the far side of the church and prepare for the attack.

He crouched again and moved forward in a low run. No one challenged him as he moved two hundred yards beyond the knoll—the church looming directly above him—and found another path that wound upward.

Slate-roofed, the bell tower of the church was a blackened stump, ruined by fire. The windows were boarded up along both sides. The building

was made of stone, parts of it dating to the four-
teenth century, according to MacMurray. For a
hundred years it had harbored only rats and the
occasional small wild animal, although Mac-
Murray had said that it had been used for a time
as a storehouse by smugglers.

Other rats occupied the ruined house of God
now; two-legged rodents as filthy and diseased
as the four-legged kind. But their disease was of
the mind and the spirit.

Keio advanced up the side of the knoll to the
top. An untended iron-fenced graveyard was on
one side, a hundred feet or more across, running
from the side of the church almost to the road.
It was filled with stone slabs, many of them top-
pled, others leaning at crazy angles.

A death ground, about to become a killing
ground.

The image satisfied Keio. It seemed fitting.

Weeds choked the graveyard. A tangled
growth of vines had taken root in the stone
walls, tendrils sprawled across the boards that
blocked the narrow, arched windows. There was
no sentry. The man on the beach had been the
only one on duty.

Keio checked his watch. The five minutes
were up. He then heard the shrill whistle of a
mortar shell rising into the night. It fell onto the
slate roof with a clatter and exploded, smashing
a hole through the slate and the wood beneath,
cracking the silence of the night.

A second whining round was already in the

air before the first had landed. Keio ran through the graveyard, vaulting the low iron fence and pulling a pin from a grenade. As the second mortar round exploded, he rose and threw the grenade. It arched through the night and fell against the steps leading to the front door of the church. Three seconds later it went off.

Someone shouted. The door of the church slapped open and a figure stumbled into the night, carrying a Kalashnikov. He choked from the smoke of the grenade and the fire of the mortars, waved a hand to clear his vision and fired at a shadow on the road.

Keio threw another grenade and unslung his Ingram as Rafael unloaded the other four mortar rounds. Fire lit up the night. As the terrorist emptied his rifle, a burst of slugs from Keio's Ingram tore him apart.

Rafael began to fire from the other side, raking the window boards. Keio threw a third grenade and ran toward the church.

Rafael continued to fire until his Ingram was empty, running parallel to the side of the church until he reached a door at the back. Terrorists poured through the door, scanning the night as their eyes adjusted to the darkness.

Rafael switched the Ingram for the Skorpion, not wanting to take time to stop and reload. On full automatic, the Skorpion fired 7.65mm cartridges at a rate of 750 rounds per minute. The Irish butchers received a blazing dose of their own medicine when they ran headlong into a volley of snarling hot lead.

Three men fell, but others appeared, leaping over their comrades' bodies, seeking cover against the raging firestorm that had shockingly rushed from the night. The Skorpion fell silent, its 20-round magazine emptied in one and a half seconds. Rafael yanked the pins from two grenades and threw them in the direction of the running men.

The first grenade exploded less than a yard in front of the terrorists fleeing from the building. They ran into the blast and the shock hurtled their bodies in the air. Shrapnel ripped through clothing and flesh, severing bone and dismembering limbs. The second grenade erupted while the mangled bodies were still airborne. Little remained of the charred, tattered corpses.

Rafael fed a fresh 32-round magazine into his Ingram and worked the bolt to chamber the first 9mm shell. He braced himself, ready to spray another volley of lethal lead across the doorway. But no more terrorists appeared, and the sacristy was filled with smoke and fire, as was the rest of the church. . . .

DAVID MCCARTER LISTENED to the firefight above his head, his eyes scanning the cellar. A tongue of flame licked at the side of the grenade box. If that box went up, the whole church would be blown sky high. And so would David McCarter.

Coughing from the effects of the smoke, he shook his head and hopped toward the table. His feet were numb but tingled coldly as he landed on his heels. He swayed and fought for his balance, refusing to fall. Then he hopped again.

Progress was slow. Flames began to eat at the wood of the box. Another hop and McCarter swayed again, then fell forward, his left shoulder brushing the box. A flicker of flame caught his hair, singeing the ends. The fire was hot against his face. His eyes stung from the heat and the smoke. Rolling with desperation across the fury of the flames, he used his body to beat out the fire inching up the box.

The wood smoked, but the fire had been snuffed. McCarter's problems were not over. Wood crackled. He knew it was only a matter of time before the fiery world above came showering down.

Wood crashed. It splintered and bulged outward as someone rammed a bench against the windows. One window broke apart, and then another. Hands reached through to pull at the boards, twisting them aside, making room for guns to appear and lay down a return fire. A third window splintered. Rafael Encizo fired as a body hurtled through the opening, clothing in flames. A scream tore through the night as the torched terrorist fell to the ground in an agonized roll of death.

The desperate defenders, taken by storm and surprise, fired through windows on both sides of the church. Flames, fed by centuries-old beams and wood dried to the condition of tinder, licked into the sky.

Keio lay down a return fire, slapped another clip in place and ran for the front of the church. MacMurray, familiar with the structure, had said that McCarter must be in the cellar. From the spread of the fire, there was little time to pull him out before the building collapsed.

He and Rafael had not come to Ireland to see their friend incinerated in the flaming ruins of a church.

As Keio broke through the front, Rafael smashed through the sacristy. For a moment the Phoenix Force agents stared into the hell that was the center of the church and almost mistook each other for the enemy. Then the real enemy turned from the windows and snapped shots across the once-hallowed nave.

Rafael and Keio turned as though motivated by one mind, Keio firing to the left, Rafael to the right. The terrorists fired back, but they had been trained to ambush and kill unsuspecting civilians, not to fight armed opponents in open combat. Putting bombs in baby carriages in Belfast or Dublin, or shooting a British policeman in the back with a rifle, were not the same as going up against a pair of warriors such as Rafael and Keio.

Keio raised his Ingram and stitched an Irish goon from crotch to throat with 9mm death. The terrorist next to the man was splattered by blood and intestinal gore. He recoiled in horror and hastily pulled the trigger of his M-45. The bullets from the Swedish chatterbox tore into the floorboards near Keio. The Japanese blasted a short volley into the terrorist's chest, chopping heart and lungs into useless pulp.

The Cuban fired a burst of 9mm slugs at another pair of Emerald Isle trash. One man's skull exploded in a nova of blood and brains. The other terrorist, a giant of a man, hurled his empty AK-47 aside and let out a roar as he rushed the altar and Rafael.

Rafael's gun was empty. The madman blundered through the flames and smoke, unmindful of the elements of hell that surrounded him. Rafael clawed for the Beretta in his shoulder leather—too late. Eamon O'Bannon was already upon him.

The big Irishman launched himself at Rafael and collided with the Cuban warrior. Both men fell heavily against the altar. They struggled fiercely, bare hands their only weapons. Rafael rammed a knee into his opponent's groin. O'Bannon merely grunted and grabbed Rafael's throat. He pushed the Cuban backward across the altar, determined to squeeze the life out of him.

Desperately Rafael clawed his fingers into O'Bannon's face. He hooked a thumb into the corner of the Irishman's left eye and gouged hard. O'Bannon shrieked when his eyeball popped out of its socket and dangled loosely on his cheek, hanging by the stem of its optic nerve. The Irishman released Rafael and fell backward, clawing at his face, still screaming in pain and horror.

The Cuban's hand dived to the Mark IV commando knife clipped to his belt. Breaking the thumb snap, he quickly drew the knife and lunged forward. Rafael executed a fast, expert lunge and drove the point of the razor-sharp double-edged blade into the hollow of O'Bannon's throat. Rafael twisted the blade, creating a larger cavity in his adversary's flesh, and then yanked the knife free.

O'Bannon staggered, one hand gripping his torn throat, the other still clamped over the empty socket. The shock and loss of blood drained the big man of his maniacal strength. He fell heavily, crashing through the remains of the communion rail. He was dead when he hit the floor; as dead as the boys who had served as his honor guard; as dead as the others who had gathered at the church in this time of danger. A dozen men were enough to stand against any opposing force of men that did not outnumber their ranks. Against any. . . .

But not against Phoenix Force.

Rafael rose to his feet as Keio ran toward him.

"David!" Keio shouted.

"The cellar!" said Rafael. He looked around then spotted a door that led off from the sacristy. "There!"

Keio ran and tugged open the door. Smoke swirled into his face, filling his lungs. There was fire below but the stairs were clear. He took them two at a time. Keio peered through the smoke-filled room. He heard his name over the roar of the fire.

"Keio! Over here!"

Through the choking haze, Keio saw McCarter kneeling behind a table—a table that was on fire. He crossed the cellar at a weaving run, doging obstacles and avoiding leaping flames.

"Damn!" said McCarter, greeting his friend. "Just like Superman. You wait to come in at the last minute. Cut me loose."

Keio saw that McCarter was tied. He reached for his knife, then part of the ceiling collapsed in a sheet of flames.

The flames were at the far end of the cellar. Keio forgot the knife. There was no time to cut David loose. He would not be able to move his strangled limbs in time.

Keio cast the Ingram aside and bent, tugging McCarter to his feet. Keio then hoisted him across his shoulders, staggering under McCarter's weight, and turned toward the stairs.

The fire had reached the stairs.

"You'll never make it!" McCarter shouted.

Keio ignored him, moving into a shambling run. The heat was intense, the smoke dense. Fire shot at Keio's legs as he started up the burning stairs. He had to turn sideways to maneuver McCarter through the narrow opening that had been left in the floor to accommodate the staircase.

Keio transported McCarter to the top of the staircase. The church was filled with smoke and fire. He looked around for Rafael but could not find his fighting friend. He had no time left to look—the church roof was collapsing.

Keio took three lurching steps that carried him across the sacristy to the back door of the church, pushed through and stumbled down three stone steps to the ground level. The church had become a torch, fire escaping through every opening. The heat was intense as he hit the ground and staggered beneath the burden of his Phoenix Force companion.

Keio ran, summoning his last reserve of strength, heading away from the burning church. He threaded through the gravestones, reached the iron fence and dumped David into the waiting arms of Rafael, just as the box of grenades in the cellar exploded.

What was left of the roof was blasted straight up. The thick walls of the old church trembled with the fury of the blast but held it contained. Debris and embers fell in a hellish rain as Keio rolled across the iron fence and fell to the ground. Hot embers struck him as he let himself roll down the hill. Sparks struck at his face and stuck in his hair, which smoldered. An ember lodged in the small of his back, burned itself out in the combat suit as he came to a halt. For a moment he lay on his back, staring into a sky turned red. Yet even as he looked, the glow subsided and the rain of debris ended. He brushed his hands through his hair, beating out the embers. He sat up, breathing raggedly, as Rafael used his knife to cut McCarter's bonds.

"About bloody time, mates," McCarter said with a grin. "Damn good work."

McCarter began to laugh. He pounded his fists against the ground. He was happy to be alive. Rafael watched him a moment, his face split in a grin.

"Well, hotshot?" Rafael said, staring at David. "What are you waiting for? There's work to be done. This war has just begun."

16

FIVE MEN WERE GATHERED in the kitchen of a flat on New York's Lower East Side. A sixth man stood guard at the door and another stood by the window in the front room, staring down at the street four floors below. There were other men sleeping in other rooms.

"Twenty-four hours and not a word," Cavan Coakley said, his brow furrowed with worry. "We know they have the letters. But not a word on television or in the newspapers. Not a word."

"The government is trying to hide the truth from the people," Seamus Riley said. He was the only terrorist who seemed calm and in control.

"They should be responding to us!" said Emmett Farrell. Liam Clune and Doyle MacGrew were the other two men at the table.

"Yes," said MacGrew. "We want to know if they're going to pay the billion dollars."

"They don't intend to pay it," Riley informed them.

"Then why in God's name are we playin' this farce?"

Liam Clune slapped his hand down on the table, and the front legs of his chair came down with a thump that startled the guard at the door.

"They won't pay," Riley repeated. "That is, until the first bomb goes off. Then they'll have no choice but to pay."

A sick look crossed Liam Clune's face. A hundred dead in the original raids, two hundred more in the bombing in California. How many would die when they set off an atomic bomb? A hundred thousand; that was the number in Hiroshima. But these warheads had fourteen times the power. Clune shuddered.

"The bombs are in place," said Riley. "Which city shall be the first target?"

"The cities are as chosen, Seamus?" Mac-Grew asked.

"They are, Doyle. There's been no reason to change the selection. We want all of the country to know about Seamus Riley and his cause."

"I was just thinking that Los Angeles...." MacGrew turned over a hand. "They've had the one bombing. They should be ready to listen to reason."

"They're not ready," Riley countered. "If they were ready, the companies would have been forced to pay. No, they listen but they don't believe. They won't believe, until we show them that they *must* believe."

"Los Angeles," said Farrell. "And Chicago."

"New York City," said Liam.

"And Washington, D.C.," finished Riley.

"Washington can't be the first," Coakley reasoned. "If we blow up the only people who can make the payment, we'll never see the money."

"No," agreed Riley, "Washington will be the last shot in our war. It will be our dyin' statement. If it comes to that, I'll be with the bomb when it goes off."

"New York," said Coakley, head hanging. "Chicago. Los Angeles."

"Which?" asked Riley.

"New York is biggest," said Liam. "The most would die here. I say it should be next to last."

"I agree," said Riley. "Chicago, or Los Angeles?"

"Chicago is concentrated, like New York," Coakley said. "It's also the rail center for the country and has the biggest port on the Great Lakes. I say first strike has to be Los Angeles."

"Does anyone object?"

Riley looked at each in turn as he asked the question. Clune studied his hands, clenched on the edge of the table. Doyle MacGrew met his eyes, glanced furtively away. Emmett Farrell leaned back, stared at the glass globe of the kitchen light.

"Then Los Angeles it is," Riley pronounced. "Which brings up another question that I'll throw before you. Do we announce the target? Or wait until the bomb goes off and announce that Chicago, New York and Washington will go in turn?''

"If we tell them, there'll be mass confusion as they try to evacuate the city," said Coakley.

"If we tell them," said MacGrew, "the locals will force the government in Washington to act. They'll have to pay the ransom."

"We'll have to be sure that this time the message gets out," said Farrell. "To the people."

"What do you say to that, Cavan?" asked Riley. "You're our public-relations expert."

Coakley flushed. "There are seventy or eighty local radio stations in Los Angeles and Orange County," he said, "fifteen or twenty local newspapers. We send the message to all of them. They will pass it on."

"We haven't got time for a full-scale press release," Farrell said.

"No," Riley agreed. "The men in Los Angeles will have to call each station and newspaper personally. That would give each ten or twelve calls to make. Do you have lists ready, Cavan?"

"They can take them out of the yellow pages for the various towns," said Coakley. "There's a supply of them all in the area command post." He stood, pushing back his chair. "I'll call them now. The word should be out within two hours."

"Make the call from a pay phone," advised Riley.

"Of course," said Coakley. "I'll use the booth in the subway. It's most secure."

Coakley took a jacket from a closet while the guard checked the peephole in the door. Riley beamed at the men at the table as Cavan slipped through the door and moved quickly down the stairs. The guard at the front window watched him turn up his collar against a sharp wind off the East River. He then hurried to the corner, turned and disappeared from sight.

The subway station was almost empty at this hour. Cavan cast a warning scowl at two hungry-eyed Hispanic teenagers, who looked at him as possible meat for the slaughter, and slipped into the phone booth. He lifted the receiver and heard the dial tone. He dropped the coin, gave the operator the Los Angeles number, fed more coins as directed and let the instrument three thousand miles away ring three times before he hung up.

He opened the booth and stepped out. The teenagers moved closer. Cavan drew his pistol from the back of his trousers and flashed it. They backed off and jumped onto the next train that came in. He began to pace, occasionally glancing at his watch, but he always stayed close to the booth.

Twelve minutes passed before the phone rang. Cavan caught it before the first ring finished and spoke four words: "The lion is dead."

It was the recognition code; it meant orders

were coming. The man in Los Angeles gave his name and listened. He repeated the instructions when Cavan finished.

"Speed counts," said Cavan. "But spread your men out. Security is still paramount."

The man in L.A. acknowledged the orders and hung up.

The Fury Bomb was set to be unleashed.

17

THREE MILES NORTH and slightly west of the railroad flat that served as the New York City headquarters for the Army of the People's Republic of Ireland, five men were gathered in a luxury suite in the Essex House hotel.

David McCarter sprawled across a French Empire sofa. His face was marked, and one eyebrow was almost gone. His left hand was bandaged. A short haircut had repaired the damage the fire had done to his hair, and a hard head had lessened the effects of the concussion that had kept him in darkness in the cellar of the Irish church.

At first look, McCarter seemed to be ripe for a long bout of R&R. But, first looks are deceptive. When terrorists were shoving, McCarter pushed his body to outer limits. R&R, in McCarter's mind, was not needed. In fact, he stressed, it was "out of the bleedin' question."

His head might have a few lumps and his wrist and ankles might be chafed raw from the ropes that had bound him, but David McCarter was still able. Very able.

McCarter tilted a can of cola, drained it and

crumpled the can in one hand. He tossed it toward a wastebasket. The can hit the rim and fell in. A sudden belch escaped and McCarter covered his mouth with a fist.

"Bloody good shot," he said, smiling. With McCarter's crass sense of humor, he could have been referring to the burp, or the basket he made with the can.

His companions laughed, glad their fighting friend was alive.

Keio Ohara also carried the scars of the church battle. A lock of hair was missing from one temple and small burn marks tattooed his face. He sat erect in a wing chair, his battle-bruised ribs aching slightly.

Yakov sat, waiting patiently. His artificial hand rested on the table, surprisingly lifelike; flesh-colored plastic-covered stainless steel, the plastic implanted with a scattering of black human hair.

The hand's steel fingers were slightly curled, resting naturally. When the fingers were locked straight, the hand was a two-pound sledge, capable of smashing any wood-paneled door. A glancing side blow could tear off a man's ear. A forward chop, against the sternum, could paralyze heart and lungs, kill.

Anticipating a need to kill without noise had led Yakov to select this tool of silent death. Yakov turned his disability into a lethal advantage.

Rafael stood at the window, looking down at

Central Park. In early afternoon, the park on the Fifth Avenue side was crowded with pedestrians even though the day was chilly and overcast. Tourists were out in force in the place that had been built as a haven for the city-weary.

A horse-drawn carriage moved slowly into the park, irritating drivers who were stuck behind it. Rafael watched until the carriage and its pair of lovers disappeared, then he turned back to the room. An ugly white mark, remnants of a blister on an earlobe, was his only visible souvenir of the burning church.

Gary impatiently paced. Finally the bedroom door opened, and Hal Brognola and another man entered the room.

"We've got it!" said Brognola exultantly, chomping heavily on an unlit cigar.

"In Los Angeles?" Gary asked, wheeling.

"Yes. Heffernan's informant pinpointed the bomb to a warehouse near Union Station. There are six men guarding the warehouse. We can take them anytime we want to. Anytime we have to."

"But we're going to wait," said Yakov.

"The Man bought everything we worked out. Unless Heffernan's man calls back with word that zero hour has been advanced, we'll wait until the guards evacuate."

Cormick Heffernan, a leader in the council of the Provisional Irish Republican Army, the Provos, was the seventh man in the room. After rescuing McCarter and returning to Belfast, Keio insisted on another meeting with Girvin Kearney, their informant.

"Cormick will never do it!" said Kearney, shocked at the proposal. "My boss go to New York? You're daft!"

"You've heard the story of the firefight at the church." Rafael smiled, showing his teeth. His voice was a silky purr that suggested inescapable menace. Kearney shivered and looked at Inspector MacMurray. He found no sympathy there.

"That little fight was my Japanese friend and myself," Rafael said, "against a dozen. We took O'Bannon like walking through a Sunday school. Now there's three of us and there are more we can call in. Does Heffernan want trouble? Does he want us to switch our attention from Seamus Riley?"

"I'll speak to him," said Kearney, scowling. "But he won't be pleased."

The ferret-faced little Irishman scuttled out of the pub like a roach scurrying for safety. He returned in less than an hour. Within twenty minutes Cormick Heffernan arrived, guarded by a dozen bully boys. He frowned as he listened to Rafael, and he scowled as he studied the Japanese and the Englishman.

Cormick was a man of middle size but had ham fists, big feet and a twisted face that gave him the look of a mean mobster. A steelworker for the Belfast shipyards until fired by his

British employers for IRA activities, Heffernan was exceedingly ugly but soft-spoken.

"Will you come?" Rafael asked, his voice demanding.

"For what purpose?"

"To use the men you have planted in Riley's army to get us information," said Keio.

"And what makes you think I have men with Seamus Riley?"

"You'd be a fool not to have them," Keio said.

Heffernan scowled. The corners of his already twisted mouth moved.

"Okay, I'll do it. And why not?" He pounded the table. "I've got a brother in Boston I've not seen in thirty years. Nine kids he has and none of them knowin' their uncle. They say the wee ones are the spittin' image of me sainted father."

Four hours had passed since Cavan Coakley's call to Los Angeles. Two hours since the bomb threat had been revealed to the public over a university FM station.

Within the hour, half the stations in L.A. repeated the warning. Like a grass fire fanned by a stiff breeze, the news had spread nationwide.

There was no longer any hope of concealing the existence of the stolen warheads.

The bedroom of the Essex House suite had been converted to a command post, furniture removed and a radio communication center established. Banks of telephones had been installed, including a direct line to Stony Man and another to the White House.

Brognola shut the door as he came out of the bedroom to cut off the noise made by the anti-terrorist experts and technicians working there. News could be relayed instantly, but the living-room suite served as a think tank for Phoenix Force, a place where they could concentrate on the movements of the terrorists—and try to outguess what Riley would do next.

"Are you sure you can trust your man?" David asked.

"He was *my* man before he was Riley's," said Heffernan stiffly. He resented the presence of the Englishman and made no effort to conceal his hatred.

"I sent him with Riley," he added, "knowing the Provos had to stay in close touch with any scheme he was proposing."

"And the other factions," said Brognola.

Heffernan lifted a shoulder. "The other factions can look out for themselves. It's the Provos who are fighting the real war and bearing the brunt of it."

While Phoenix Force members monitored Riley and planned their course of action, the city of Los Angeles was erupting in a state of panic. The freeways were clogged in all directions, city streets a mad circus as frightened drivers ran traffic lights in the hope of gaining an advantage over the next car. The populace was fleeing frantically with no destination in mind. They were fleeing the bomb.

Some, with foresight, were prepared and had loaded their cars and trucks and vans with canned goods and blankets, cans of water and gasoline, rifles and handguns. A few were pragmatic, prepared for any emergency from earthquake to fire to mudslides that could seal off canyon roads for days or weeks. Others were survivalists, ready to shoot down neighbor or friend if it helped them to live.

Still others, less practical and panic-stricken, grabbed whatever they could before leaving their homes.

Those who lived in the marinas and had boats and yachts headed out to sea. Others, less fortunate economically, stole transportation that ranged from those same marina boats to custom Excalibur automobiles to small planes, and even city buses.

In the chaos of evacuation, looting had started. Watts was near riot. Every off-duty city policeman and sheriff's deputy had been called in, along with the civilian reserves. Many were still struggling to reach their duty stations. Others had joined the exodus.

The mayors of Los Angeles and Santa Monica, Pasadena and Long Beach, Anaheim and Ventura and Torrance and the other incorporated cities of Los Angeles and the surrounding counties were on the panic line to Sacramento, demanding that the governor send out the National Guard.

The governor was on another line, to Washington, pleading to get the same guard released from the federalization alert called when the first threat of the Irish terrorists surfaced.

North, south and east, the mass of panic-stricken people surged, heading for the supposed safety of the hills, the high desert, Palm Springs, the Sierras, Mexico, Las Vegas.

The evacuation and the looters were civil problems. If Seamus Riley was not stopped, such civil problems would be stifled in the rage of a nuclear blast. The civil problems could wait.

They would have to wait.

Phoenix Force concentrated on Riley.

They were looking for the three remaining bombs.

"What's the plan?" McCarter asked.

"We figure the guards in the warehouse will evacuate at least three hours before zero hour," said Hal Brognola. "Probably earlier, considering the problem they've given themselves of getting out of there."

"Assuming they're not suicidal like the one who blew himself apart with his grenade in Chicago," said Rafael.

"We have to make that assumption," said Hal. "They must have escape routes prepared. They need men to continue their 'war.' You agree, Heffernan?"

The Irishman shrugged. "If raided, they would set off the bomb and die. But they're not fools. Lives are not to be thrown away needlessly. Riley needs men for his army."

Brognola nodded. "We'll go in as soon as they leave and neutralize the bomb. We'll have tails on the guards. There's a slim chance they'll lead us to Riley, or at least to the other bombs."

"Unlikely," said Yakov. "He has his army well compartmented. Each group seems to know only what it must know to carry out its function."

"Riley knows what he's doing," said Heffernan. "The man may be crazy, but he's also cagey."

"There's a stronger possibility the guards will try to report to Riley," said Brognola. "We've got our people in Washington—with a little help from our friends at the phone company—doing a little tapping in the area. If they make a call, we'll know about it."

"What about the bomb itself?" Gary Manning asked Heffernan. "Is it on a timer, or will it be set off by remote control?"

"My man knows nothing about the firing device," said Heffernan. "Only the guy who actually armed the bomb knows that."

"It's probably a combination of the two," said Manning. "If it fails to go off on the timer, there'll be a backup. It's unlikely it would be radio controlled—I'd do it by telephone. They're easy to work by phone—you call twice, or even three times. Let it ring twice, three times, and then the second or third call fires the bomb.''

"We'd take the bomb now," Brognola said, "but if Riley is alerted he'll just switch to one of the backups."

"We don't know where those bastard bombs are," McCarter said.

"One's got to be in New York," Yakov said.

"Washington," added Manning.

"They're going for the biggest cities," said Keio. "It's only logical. They are trying to punish the United States for not forcing the companies to give in to the original demand."

"Houston or Chicago," said Rafael. "It's probably one of those, along with New York and Washington."

The bedroom door opened. A man in shirtsleeves and suspenders stood there, necktie pulled loose from his collar.

"Riordan's come back to his apartment," he said. "From the sounds we're pickin' up on the bugs, he doesn't intend to stay very long. He might just have a meeting planned with his old buddy Riley."

The Phoenix Force agents moved into the other room. A map of Manhattan showing the streets and major reference points from the Battery to Central Park was covered with a plastic overlay, marked with pins and grease pencils. Another showed the city from 42nd Street to the

South Bronx, and others covered the other boroughs and Long Island.

A technician held up a hand. "Riordan's leaving the apartment. Heading for Sixth Avenue."

More than a minute passed as reports were relayed by the full team of city and federal agents that had been spotted on Riordan. The others waited in silence.

"He just went into the subway, the uptown IND on the side."

The Phoenix Force antiterrorists broke for the other room, scooping up outer wear and radios that would keep them in communication with the command post. Brognola and Heffernan stayed behind.

Every possibility had been covered. Two men would be on the subway car with Riordan, two more in each adjoining car.

Teams of men had the subway system blanketed, while others covered bus terminals, airports.... If Riordan tried to leave town, rent a car, buy a magazine or breath, he would be covered.

But they hoped he stayed in Manhattan; Riordan was important to Phoenix Force and their New York City helpers only if he led them to Riley, his Irish gang and the bombs. If he left Manhattan, if he skipped the country, he was just a lead that died before it blossomed.

The Phoenix Force members separated as

they hit 59th Street and spread out to cover the most likely routes Riordan could choose.

Gary Manning sprinted for an unmarked car that would be in contact with the command post in the Essex House.

For two days Gary Manning had been chasing shadows, trying to capture clues while the other Phoenix Force agents tasted action. He was not a watcher. He yearned for the fight. And Riordan was his meat. His hunch about Ames Computronics in Sussex had been wrong, but he would make up for that. He would even the score.

18

GARY MANNING piled into the back seat of the unmarked car, which was already manned by two New York City plainclothes detectives. But there was no place to go. In a moment the radio, tuned to a special channel that received the reports by the teams on Riordan, crackled to life.

"Subject entered A train, headed uptown."

Time passed, minutes dragged.

"Subject left train at 42nd Street. Now he's headed for exit. Moving toward Port Authority."

Manning followed Riordan's every move with the aid of the radio.

Riordan left the subway train at 42nd Street then entered the Port Authority bus terminal, meandering along, stopping to purchase a dozen donuts.

"Donuts, for God's sake," retorted one of the cops in Manning's car when he heard that report. "Donuts...."

From there Riordan reentered the subway and moved toward the tunnel to Times Square. He then caught the shuttle, took the short crosstown trip and headed for Grand Central, out onto Lexington Avenue then cut north and east along 48th Street.

"Subject just entered 866 UN Plaza," came the report from a cop tail.

"What's there?" Manning asked.

Hal Brognola's booming voice answered the question over the radio. "That's the Libyan Mission. His wife works in the building."

Manning's impatience grew. "Head toward the Mission," he told the driver. The driver obeyed, but crosstown traffic was sluggish.

"Subject just left Mission with a woman," the voice said, returning after a short silence. "Women is in her late forties, dumpy, dyed brown hair."

"That's his wife," Cormick Heffernan's voice interjected.

Neal Riordan hailed a cab. He then bundled his wife into the cab, gave the driver instructions and left his wife with a quick wink and a smile.

Brognola's voice boomed again. "Someone follow the damn cab. God only knows what his wife is up to."

"We've got the cab covered by helicopter, Hal," said a New York cop who was helping coordinate the tail. "Looks like it's headed for the 59th Street Bridge."

Meanwhile, Riordan had reached 50th Street, crossing Second Avenue.

Gary Manning heard this update and he felt the pent-up frustration explode. He busted out

of the back seat of the unmarked car and
hollered as he took off: "I'll keep on the
bastard by foot."

Manning, bumping bodies, ignoring glares,
stares and curses, kept the radio held to his ear
as he stormed after Riordan.

"Subject crossing Lexington. Subject entering downtown entrance to subway."

As the voice died, Manning reached the subway station, the breath ripped from his lungs.
He pounded down the stairs. Hitting the bottom, he looked about as three other agents came
barreling down other stairways.

Riordan, unaware of the tails, stood at the
south end of the train station, near where the
first car of the train would stop. Stepping
behind a crowd of commuters, Manning reported in.

"Manning. I have the subject."

The train rumbled in from the north. Manning entered the same car as Riordan. The Irishman snatched a seat away from a tall woman
in a miniskirt. Manning leaned against a steel
post.

The subway train entered Grand Central and
discharged most of its passengers. Manning
surveyed the train as it rumbled along. It was
filthy, its walls and windows smeared with graf-
fiti, its seats scarred and gouged by vandals.

The train passed under the east side of the
island and came to a stop at the Brooklyn
Bridge station. Riordan hopped out, followed

by Manning and the other agents who made themselves scarce as they went up the stairs.

Manning let the Irishman get a hundred feet ahead before he followed. He picked him up again at the top of the stairs. The tailing became tricky as Riordan worked his way north several blocks and then moved east, crossing Avenue A and Avenue B. But the subject seemed oblivious to the fact that he might be followed. Whistling, he turned north on Avenue C, crossed the avenue and turned east on the next block. By the time Manning reached the corner, he was mounting the stoop of a five-story tenement.

Manning continued across the corner as Riordan entered the building. The other agents had picked him up; one broke into a run to the next corner, and then turned east—he circled the block and came in from the other side. A second turned boldly onto the block, walked on the south side and showed no apparent interest in the north side of the street.

The third agent stopped, checked his watch. This part of New York was a wasteland, buildings abandoned and burned out, the people dressed in ill-fitting coats and suspicious of strangers. Several black men ambled along Avenue C, eyeing the white interlopers. Manning ignored them, his eyes searching for lookouts.

He cast a last look down the block and moved to where he could duck below a stoop. There

Manning took out the radio and reported. The other three agents did the same.

"There's a man in the fourth-floor front window."

"Another on the roof. Make that two. They're both carrying rifles."

Brognola came on. "Is there any indication Choirboy is there?"

Choirboy was the code name for Seamus Riley. Rafael Encizo had suggested it, only half facetiously, when it was learned that Riley had been a sought-after tenor during his youth.

"Nothing," said one of the other agents. "But somebody or something damn important is there."

"The bombs?" said another.

Another of the men came on. "Can't we get some better coverage? I think the guy in the window made me."

"Sit tight, it's on the way," said the commander. "Take up positions where you can watch the block even if you have to lose the building. Stay out of sight."

Brognola came back. "P-team, converge."

That was the signal for the Phoenix Force agents to come together. Manning worked the fingers of his right hand, unconsciously nodding as the various voices came on.

If Riley was in there, the bastard would not slip through his fingers this time.

Manning glanced at the sky. There was no way they could take the terrorists by day; not by a full frontal assault. They had to take them alive in a firefight.

Riley had to be alive.

They would have to wait until dark and go over the roof.

Sunset would arrive in three hours.

Three hours until wartime—New York style.

Phoenix Force style.

19

A BUM WEAVED DOWN AVENUE C, occasionally stopping to peer through litter in a trash can. He wore a filthy gray overcoat that dragged on the ground, drab army cap and dirty, torn brown cotton gloves.

He started to cross the street but stopped in the middle of the road, swaying again. He turned abruptly and staggered into an open stairwell. The bum stayed there for quite some time then started down the street. He reached no farther than two houses before he collapsed onto the stoop. For a moment he sat with knees splayed and hands between his thighs. Then he slowly folded onto his side, curled up on the step, and fell asleep.

Twenty minutes later an aging Ford Econoline van turned onto the avenue, heading north. The van's body was heavily dented, scarred and showed rust-red undercoating beneath blue paint. A bumper sticker proclaimed PUERTO RICAN POWER!

As the van drew abreast of the terrorist house, its right front tire blew. The van bumped to a stop. A Hispanic youth jumped out of the driver's side, stared at the tire then hauled off and kicked the side of the fender, shouting a loud curse.

The other door popped open and four more youths got out. The five young people gathered around the flat tire, staring, and then an argument broke out over the driver's stupidity in not having a spare.

The argument grew very loud with hands waving wildly. One of the five, a girl, grabbed one of the boys by the arm. They began to argue, the girl trying to tug him toward the corner. At last he surrendered and said they were leaving. The others followed.

The driver had been deserted. He glared at the van, kicked it again then hurried after his friends.

That left only three men hidden in the back of the van.

Traffic on Avenue C picked up. A Consolidated Edison van came to a stop at a manhole. Two men jumped out, pried up the cover and set up a circular steel fence around the hole. They brought lights and equipment from the back of the truck, lowered it into the hole and disappeared.

Gary Manning, leaving his hiding place, approached the rear door of the van. It opened. Rafael Encizo reached out, caught his hand and yanked him inside.

"Welcome, amigo," said the Cuban, grinning.

Manning stripped off his street clothing. He donned a combat suit and began to check out his weapons in the tight confines of the truck. When he finished, he settled himself to wait.

They were ready for the assault.

It was only a matter of time.

Other agents poured into the area, moving into the surrounding empty houses. At the same time the denizens of these rat dens departed for more seemly climes. Two blocks north of the terrorist house agents climbed to the roof, took up positions overlooking the target.

Reports continued to come over the radio.

The police helicopter had trailed the cab carrying Riordan's wife over the 59th Street Bridge and along Queens Boulevard to the Brooklyn-Queens Expressway. The cab stayed with the BQE until it merged with the Grand Central Parkway, headed east to La Guardia. Ground agents took over, men who had been staked out against the possibility of Riordan himself trying to leave that way. They followed her to the Eastern Airlines counter and reported she bought a one-way ticket to Miami.

"Shall we take her?" a cop asked.

"Negative," said Hal Brognola. "But stay with her to make sure she takes the flight."

Riordan's wife was unimportant. But her departure without luggage was a good indication that New York was one of the target cities.

Shortly after six o'clock Hal Brognola came

on the radio again. He could not hide the elation in his voice.

"Heffernan's informants just came in. We've pinpointed the Chicago and Washington bombs.

"I've talked to the Man. It's been decided we'll take out the bombs now. The Chicago man says the bombs are on telephone triggers. Washington and Chicago were told to clear out three hours before the L.A. bomb is due to go off. If there's a screw-up, Chicago will be fired instead, and then New York."

"Won't the terrorists fire the bombs in self-defense?" asked Keio anxiously.

"Heffernan's men say they won't have a chance. They're going back with gas grenades. Nonlethal, because they'll be knocked out themselves, but they'll do the jobs. We'll have bomb teams in there within twenty minutes, defusing them."

"But still no word on the New York bomb," said David.

"That's up to you five," said Brognola. "None of Heffernan's men are in New York. "They say Riley's holed up with only his top guns. New York's in your hands."

Dusk gathered and settled over the desolate Lower East Side. Except for the streetlights on the avenues and the twinkling red and green traffic signals, the area was dark. Black. Deserted.

Gary checked his watch. "It's time." Rafael

was paired with Gary. The two nodded at David and Keio, then moved out quickly when David opened the door. Rafael and Gary each carried an Ingram, silenced with noise suppressors. Rafael had a bag of grenades and Gary had a hunting bow and four arrows.

They moved north, two black shadows, almost invisible. They turned onto the first block north of the terrorist house, and disappeared into a deserted house.

Rafael flicked on a pencil flash and the pair advanced to the third floor. Opening the trapdoor on the roof, Rafael peered outside.

"I see one sentry at the back of the house," he whispered to Gary Manning. "His head just shows over the wall. He can't see us if we go out low."

Manning nodded. "Let's go."

Rafael made his way over the top of the trapdoor, pushing his bag of grenades ahead of him.

Manning followed and stopped at the top. He heard the slithering sound as Rafael made for the shelter of the nearest chimney. When the noise stopped, he lifted his head far enough to scan the roof.

Rafael peered around the chimney, gave a signal, then Gary went over onto the roof.

The roof was a mine field of discarded mattresses, broken glass and plastic trash bags. Gary moved toward the chimney in a crouch. He then slowly stood and moved until he could sight along the chimney cap.

The sentry was there, the upper half of his body showing above the low wall that surrounded that roof. Then another man appeared and stood beside him.

"Christ, it's cold!" said one. "I wish 'twere done an' finished. I'd rather be back in Londonderry, where a man has family and friends to watch his back, than in this godforsaken place."

"D'you think the Americans will pay?" said the other.

"Seamus said they would."

"He said the Brit companies would pay, but they didn't. Killin' their people just put their backs up, made them as stubborn as an Irishman."

Gary unslung the hunting bow, notched the cord and drew one of the arrows he carried.

The conversation on the next roof ended. Gary glanced around the chimney and saw that both sentries were moving away. He stepped out, brought the bow to position and let fly with the first arrow.

It struck the target silently. The terrorist made a small noise, hardly a protest but enough to alert his partner. The second man started to turn but was stabbed by Gary's second arrow, which tunneled through his heart.

The Irishmen dropped. Rafael sprang forward, ran to the wall and crouched to be sure the noise of their collapse had not been heard. After thirty seconds, he went over the wall, landed on the terrorists' roof and moved forward with the Ingram ready to check the trapdoor.

Rafael stood and Gary, abandoning the bow by the trapdoor, joined him. They moved to the front of the house, and signaled twice.

Across the street, the bum rolled over and sat up with a yawn. He opened his coat to scratch his chest. He did not move from his sitting position but his hand remained inside his coat, touching the folded stock of his Uzi.

In the van, the three men tensed, ready to enter the battleground from the rear doors. One man pressed the transmit button of a radio twice.

The signal was received in the Con Edison truck. The two remaining Phoenix Force agents worked gas masks over their heads.

Gary and Rafael donned gas masks as David opened the truck's door and slipped out, followed closely by Keio. The latter carried an M-16 rifle with a grenade launcher attached; a grenade was ready for firing.

They moved to the east side of the block, slipped from shadow to shadow, hugging the stoops. On the north side of the street, they could not be seen from the fourth-floor window of the terrorists' flat.

The bum watched the window. He pulled off the cap and scratched vigorously.

In the flat, the sentry held back the curtain in the front room and let it fall almost immediately. The action had become routine. He did little more than glance at the street. The abandoned van and the bum no longer bothered him.

The bum watched David move into the shadows of the terrorists' stoop and use the bars on a window to pull himself up the wall until he stood on the broad cement railing, flattened beside the door.

There was a sentry inside; that had been verified by the men in the van.

He had to be drawn out.

David signaled. The bum came off the stoop and started across the street, hitching up his pants. He stooped, looked up at the lighted window and studied the building as though wondering whether to make it his home for the night.

The glass on the doors was intact, although one of the panes on an inner door had been replaced with plywood. The bum came to a decision and started up the steps. He opened the door, moved inside and came backpedaling, hands out in protest.

"Hey now, mister! Ain't no call for that! I didn't do nothing."

"Out, you drunken bum!"

The sentry came out, cursing, ready to strike at the bum with the butt of his rifle. "Out, before I give you a taste of my...."

David struck. The blade sliced through muscle and fat, the sentry staring with astonishment as the instrument of death plunged deep. Before he could protest, David pulled the rifle from his hand and used the pull to spin him around. He clamped a hand over the sentry's mouth as blood spilled from the eighteen-inch gash, splattering across the soiled stoop.

Yakov came up the steps, shrugging out of the filthy overcoat, his Uzi ready. He worked a gas mask into place as Keio cut across the street, dropped into cover behind a stoop and raised the rifle. An instant later the grenade smashed through the fourth-floor window, and gas blossomed into the front room.

Gary and Rafael were ready. Gary's heel slammed against the door, which collapsed in, and Rafael tossed two quick grenades before the terrorists could react.

The terrorists coughed and choked on the gas. Several fell to the floor, totally immobilized, retching in agony. Others remained on their feet and retained their weapons, despite the waves of nausea and lack of muscle control created by the gas. Mucus dripped from their noses and drool slobbered from their mouths. Their bladders relaxed and urine stained the crotch of more than one pair of trousers. The terrorists' eyes burned and their lungs felt as if they were filled with red-hot needles.

Phoenix Force burst into the apartment.

Yakov, his Uzi in his left hand, the frame braced across his prosthetic right arm, literally ran into two of the fumbling, puking terrorists. Before the thugs could react, Yakov smashed into action. His right arm slashed a forearm smash to the closest man's chest, sending the Irish fanatic hurtling across the room.

The Israeli brushed aside the second terrorist's AK-47 with the frame of his Uzi and drove a knee into the startled man's groin. The terrorist doubled up with a groan, and Yakov chopped the side of his steel hand into his opponent's collarbone, shattering it as though it were made of glass. The man fell on his face, unconscious, while his partner drew a commando knife from an ankle sheath and launched himself at the Phoenix Force leader.

Rafael and Gary charged into the melee to discover two other terrorists still on their feet. One Irish bastard tried to swing a 9mm pistol toward the pair, although his trembling muscles and uncontrolable hacking cough made his efforts slow and awkward. Rafael stepped forward and delivered a roundhouse kick that sent the gun flying from the terrorist's grasp. The Cuban then backhanded the frame of his Ingram across the man's face, breaking his jawbone.

Another terrorist swung his AK-47 in a desperate butt-stroke at Gary Manning's head. The Canadian easily dodged the clumsy attack and stabbed the barrel of his M-10 under the man's rib cage. The terrorist gasped and folded at the middle. Gary's rock-hard fist landed a solid left hook to the side of his opponent's skull, and the Irishman dropped.

Yakov pivoted to face the knife-wielding terrorist. His face contorted with rage, the Irish assassin ignored the effects of the gas and delivered a murderous slash at Yakov's throat, exposed beneath the gas mask. The prosthetic arm rose swiftly and the seven-inch blade struck the steel limb, harmlessly bouncing off.

Before the stunned terrorist could react, Yakov chopped the edge of his deadly steel hand into the man's wrist, breaking bone on impact. The knife fell to the floor and the Irishman howled in agony. Yakov then jabbed the muzzle of his Uzi into the man's solar plexus. The terrorist moaned loudly and seemed to bow before the Israeli colonel, who promptly slammed a knee into the bully boy's face. The terrorist crashed to the floor without even uttering a sigh.

"Casualties?" barked Yakov, his voice distorted by the mask.

"None," said Rafael. The dead sentries did not count.

Gary drew his radio and reported briefly. By the time the gas began to clear and the masks became useless, the terrorists had been rounded up and gathered into the kitchen. There were nine of them, confused and sickened by the gas, their hands cuffed behind their backs.

Other footsteps sounded. Brognola appeared, followed by Heffernan. Hal looked at the captives, and then at the Irishman.

"Which is Riley?"

Heffernan shook his head. "None of them. Are you sure this is the lot?"

"It's everyone in the flat," said Gary.

"Search the house," said Yakov.

The agents moved out, smashed doors into other flats, frightening a few other illegal occupants. But there were no more terrorists.

They returned and reported. Brognola scowled and turned to Heffernan again.

"Do you know any of them?"

"Most of them," said Heffernan. He moved along the line. "Doyle MacGrew. Peter O'Rourke. Emmett Farrell. Liam Clune. These are Riley's lieutenants. If any know where he's hidin', it'll be them."

Brognola stared at the terrorists. "Well? Where is he?"

They would not talk.

Somewhere in the city of New York, one bomb waited for the mad last strike of the Irish war.

20

THE IRISH TERRORISTS were driven to police headquarters and interrogated by teams of agents. But the terrorists would not so much as admit they knew the name of Seamus Riley.

The evening dragged.

Doyle MacGrew would say nothing at all and shrugged when asked if he wanted coffee or food. Emmett Farrell cursed Heffernan for a traitor, and then cursed the factions when told of their action against Riley.

Peter O'Rourke seemed most vulnerable but, whether from fear or loyalty, remained true to the terrorist code of silence.

Liam Clune seemed sunk in despair.

"This is gettin' us nowhere," said Heffernan. He yawned widely and stretched to ease the tension of knotted back muscles. "They won't talk for fear of what the others will think, or what they'll do. These lads have long memories. They know what they'd do to a traitor."

"What do you suggest?" said Yakov. "We're open to any suggestion."

"Offer them a deal," said Heffernan. "Protection, a new life under a new name."

They began again, this time making the offer. It was received with disdain by the first three of Riley's lieutenants; then Liam Clune was brought into the room.

He looked up. "What deal?"

Brognola explained the provisions of the cooperative witness act.

"You won't send me back to Ireland?"

"Not if you tell us everything, your part in this affair; where Riley is hiding; the location of the bomb."

"The latter I can't tell you," said Clune. "I swear, Seamus kept that information for himself. But I can tell you where he is now."

"We're waiting," said Brognola.

"On the farm, upstate."

Clune opened up and spilled everything he knew, including the location of the Chenango County farm. He told his own part in the Britamco takeover in Atlanta. He would not stop talking until at last Yakov grew weary of his voice and cut him off.

"Enough! I am sickened! With your own hands you murdered a helpless old man and another."

"I'd give a penny to know how many Englishmen he's killed," said David, grimly.

"But I have your word!" said Clune. "A new life in a new place, that was the bargain!"

"It's as bad a bargain as ever I made," said Brognola, "but the United States government will stand by it."

"And you'll not tell the lads it was I who spilled?" insisted Clune.

"You don't think they'll guess when you turn up missing?" said Rafael.

Clune's face fell again. "Aye, they'll know. But they won't be able to find me."

The Phoenix Force agents rose as one and moved toward the door. Then Yakov stopped, looking at the weasel. His eyes shifted to his artificial hand.

The Irish terrorist shivered as he recognized the look in the Israeli's eyes. Clune's complexion was sallow, bleached of all color. He looked as though he would be sick when Yakov moved to his side, rested the steel hand against the back of his neck.

The fingers were in natural position but it would be easy to take Clune's spinal cord between thumb and forefinger. A slight exertion and the steel fingers would crush the cord as easily as snapping a twig....

Yakov blinked. He had almost done it.

He could not kill Clune so casually, without the excuse of battle. That would make him no better than the terrorists.

"You're coming with us," he said.

Face white, Liam Clune rose from his chair and moved after the five agents.

21

A CABLEVISION SERVICE TRUCK drove along a narrow rural lane, the man in the passenger's seat working his way through an apple. As the truck drew abreast of a long dirt driveway, he tossed the apple core from the window. Neither driver nor passenger paid special attention to the white house that sat back nearly a quarter of a mile from the road.

The farmhouse was isolated, standing five hundred yards from the road, across a field gone to seed. The windows were boarded up, the barn shut up. A rusting cultivator sagged behind a chicken coop, and weeds grew in the driveway. The house had two cars parked on the lawn and a station wagon in the driveway. A panel truck was pulled up close to the back porch, almost touching the steps. Shades were pulled tight on all windows.

"Too bad they didn't rent the big house," said David. "Plenty of cover. No cover at all where they are."

"It'll be like a turkey shoot," Gary agreed.

"No problem if we could wait until dark," said David as the truck passed the next three deserted farms. Three miles north of the tenant farmhouse the truck finally passed an occupied house.

"No time," said Gary. "It's now or never."

In one hour the Los Angeles bomb was due to explode.

Time was ticking toward action.

Gary turned into the yard of the one occupied house, which had been taken over as a command center. The farmer and his family were being kept happy in a nearby town.

"Well?" said Yakov when David and Gary entered the farmhouse. "Any ideas?"

"A bombing raid," David said. "The bloody house sits there with a quarter-mile open land on all sides. According to Clune, there are at least twenty men inside. Drop a bomb down the chimney and pick up the pieces."

"If we could get a chopper there, I could drop a gas grenade down the chimney," said Rafael.

"No," said Yakov, "they won't let a chopper or a plane get within striking distance."

"We have to do something quick," said Keio. "Time's running out."

"There's always the old underground railroad station," said the sheriff. The Phoenix Force agents spun staring at him.

"That's the second house on that foundation," explained the lawman. "First one burned down twenty-five years ago. It dated back to the Civil War and was a regular stop on the underground railroad runnin' slaves to Canada. Used to be a barn with a springhouse thirty or forty feet back of the present house. It had a well with a tunnel that ran to the woodlot.''

"Is the tunnel still there?'' asked Yakov.

"Yah,'' said the sheriff. "Buddy of mine lived on the farm for a couple of years. We used to play in it. It's kinda tight, maybe four feet, four feet and a few inches high, big enough for one man to move in, but it's stout-built, big planks on the walls and the roof.''

"Where does the tunnel come out?''

"In an old sugarin'-off shack about a hundred feet inside the woods. I ain't been there in twenty years, mind, the shack's probably fallen in by now.''

"Can we reach the woods without being seen from the house?''

"Come cross-country. Maybe a half mile from the state road. Marshy there. Once you're in the woods the ground's dry.''

"Well?'' Yakov scanned the other agents. "Does anyone have a better idea?''

"I say go for it!'' said Gary.

"I agree,'' said Rafael. David and Keio indicated assent at the same time.

Forty minutes remained until the deadline.

IN THE FARMHOUSE, Seamus Riley glanced at a clock on the mantel and checked it against his watch.

"Forty minutes, lads,'' he said.

"They're not payin', Seamus,'' said the man

who had been the electrician in the Atlanta raid. A television set flickered in a corner of the room. In the kitchen, one man sat at the table, listening to the local radio station, waiting for a news bulletin.

"Don't worry. They'll pay tomorrow," said Riley. "They'll have to pay tomorrow."

"Forty minutes," he repeated.

The sheriff's cars ferried the Phoenix Force agents to the state road.

"The telephone company is ready?" asked Yakov.

"Right," said the sheriff. "They'll wait until he makes the call to Los Angeles then kill the line."

"There may be two or three calls," Yakov reminded him.

"They know. They'll give up to a minute between them."

The Phoenix Force team moved into the field, which was waist high in grass and wild clover. Weapons held high, they pushed through the grass.

Within a hundred feet they were ankle-deep in water; the woods were still two hundred yards away. The five men broke through the obstacles, shoes filling with water and picking up layers of mud, their breath whistling from open mouths and nostrils.

Nearly fifteen minutes passed before they reached the woods; the last twenty yards was dry land. They slipped into the wood lot, and the going became easy despite heavy under-brush.

They reached the sugaring-off shack. One wall of the structure had collapsed, the roof sagging to form a trough that held an inch of rainwater. The underbrush had taken over the clearing and leaf mold was heavy underfoot.

Keio and David kicked through the mold that had drifted through the open side of the shack. Keio found rotten boards with his third kick. He dropped to his knees and pulled them apart; they broke in his hands. They were wet and heavy with mold. He shone his flashlight into the black hole and spotted the bones of small animals scattered over the bottom.

"Something has made this a home," he said.

"A fox," said Gary. "Maybe a raccoon."

"There's a ladder," said Keio, "but it looks rotten."

"Who goes through?" said David. "Who stays on top?"

Keio jumped into the hole. The lair stank of its former owner, but it seemed empty. He shone the torch into the tunnel.

"It still seems sound," he said.

Gary jumped, landing in a crouch. Rafael came after. David looked at Yakov and shrugged.

"I guess we're elected to go over the bloody top."

Yakov lowered bags of grenades, clips of extra ammunition, Ingrams and Rafael's Skorpion. Keio shouldered the M-16 with its grenade launcher attached.

"How much time?" asked Gary, burdened.

"Ten minutes," Yakov said from above.

"Let's get the hell moving," Gary said.

Yakov and David stayed by the hole just long enough to see the three agents disappear into the tunnel, Gary first, followed by Keio then Rafael. They bent low to enter the opening and then were gone. The remaining two men set out through the woods at a dogtrot, intending to reach the edge and be set up well before the others could reach the exit at the well.

Gary's load brushed the plank sides of the tunnel as he moved forward, the bright beam of his flashlight picking out the trail. The tunnel still seemed sound, although small piles of dirt had filtered through cracks.

In the middle, Keio felt the pressure of the ground bearing down on him from above. He felt the walls pressing in on either side. It was unfamiliar, frightening. He had never known claustrophobia. He heard the labored breathing of the others and fought to keep panic from blowing his heart to abnormal size. One foot in front of the other, ignore the darkness, keep eyes on Gary's back.

The tunnel opened into a circular chamber about eight feet across. Walled with stone, it narrowed as it rose to the roof, out of sight overhead.

It was the well. Gary straightened and eased

the kinks out of back and leg muscles. The others did the same as he shone the light on the well's cover. It was ten feet over their heads; the opening above was no more than three feet across.

The well was dry. There was no indication it had ever been filled with water. A wood ladder stood against the wall, but it was rotten; the bottom rung split away from handmade nails when Rafael tested it with his weight. The ladder was useless.

Keio shrugged out of his burden and bent. Gary did the same and stepped onto Keio's back and then his shoulders. His hands waved as Keio slowly straightened, until he could reach one of the planks.

According to the sheriff, the well was two feet or more above ground, but a century of drifted dirt and debris had raised the ground level around the circular wall. Gary moved a plank and dirt showered down, filling his hair and face and mouth.

He spit it away and brushed a hand across his face as Keio grunted under the dirt and strain. Gary pushed the plank to one side. Rising cautiously, he looked out at the back of the house. He moved another plank and held onto the lip of the well with both hands.

"Closed up tight," he said. "Shades drawn on every window. Van is still by back porch."

He looked down. "Give me my Ingram. I'm going to make a move for the van."

Rafael handed up the weapon, and Gary slung it over one shoulder. Keio moved beneath his shifting weight. Gary grabbed the lip of the well again to save himself from falling, then went up and out, shoulders knocking the planks farther aside and starting a new rain of dirt.

At the edge of the woods, Yakov and David saw Gary emerge from the well, move in a crouching run that carried him to the van. He dropped flat against the ground and rolled under the van. He stayed there thirty seconds before he rolled out again. Rafael peered from the well.

Gary signaled and Rafael came out. He turned back to take weapons from Keio, then leaned over to give Keio a hand. Gary crouched beside the van, the truck between him and the house. Rafael and Keio joined him. They hugged the wall, keeping below the line of the windows.

SEAMUS RILEY had picked up the telephone. He'd dialed the number of a telephone in the warehouse near Union Station in Los Angeles and listened to the instrument ring three times before he hung up. He redialed immediately.

In the warehouse, the telephone rang twice, then one of the government agents had lifted the instrument and hit the cutoff button. Riley heard the interrupted ring, followed by the hum of an open circuit. He'd let the receiver drop into its cradle and turned with a smile to the others.

"It's done, lads. Let's have the news."

The TV and radio were turned up. The men gathered in the two rooms.

Five minutes passed and no news.

Ten minutes passed.

The television and the radio continued with normal programming. The terrorists eyed one another uneasily.

"Something's wrong," said Cavan Coakley. "There should have been a bulletin by now."

Scowling, Riley spun around and picked up the telephone. He held it to his ear, ready to dial another number.

"The instrument is dead!" he said.

In that same instant, windows smashed and grenades rolled into the kitchen and the dining room.

Fire blossomed and men screamed against the noise. They staggered through the smoke, those who were still on their feet, and caught up weapons. The terrorists turned to fire at the windows as the front and back doors simultaneously were blown out by Gary and David. Seconds later the Phoenix Force agents leaped the curtain of fire and poured into the house, sending a hail of steel-jacketed death that tore through walls, fractured furniture into splinters the size of toothpicks, turned flesh and blood into pulpy masses of gore.

Rafael hit the floor in a rapid shoulder roll,

coming up on one knee, his Ingram M-10 spraying 9mm destruction that pitched two terrorists into hell. Gary blasted another Irish rebel before the man could work the bolt of his assault rifle. David's M-10 exploded with a tongue of orange fire that churned a fourth killer's chest into a bloodied mess. Another Irishman tried to bring his gun into play, but Yakov's Uzi cut his backbone in two before the man could squeeze the trigger.

A startled terrorist panicked and literally threw his AK-47 at Keio Ohara when the weapon jammed. The tactic was so stupid and unexpected, it worked. The Russian-made rifle knocked Keio off guard and hit the Ingram from his grasp.

However, Keio reacted immediately. Before the Irishman could follow up his attack, Keio leaped forward, his body rocketing across the room, one leg extended in a flying side kick. The bottom of his boot crashed into the terrorist's face, snapping his head back with such force that vertebrae popped.

The terrorist fell, his neck broken. Keio nimbly landed on his feet beside a large armchair behind which another Irish terrorist cowered.

The terrorist was still stunned and disoriented by the explosions that had signaled the assault, but he still had enough wits left to draw a .38 Smith & Wesson from its holster as he rose to face Keio.

The Japanese warrior was far faster than his adversary. His left hand shot out and caught the Irishman's wrist, pulling the gun toward the ceiling. The revolver roared and a .38 slug punched into plaster above their heads. Keio's right hand seized the man's pistol and twisted it from his grasp. With a roar of rage, the terrorist tried to throw a punch with his free hand, but Keio suddenly rammed a karate *empi* stroke to the hardguy's armpit, his elbow striking the nerve center at the subaxillary bundle.

The Irishman gasped and convulsed from the paralyzing blow. Keio's left hand swung a *shuto* chop under the terrorist's breastbone. The man groaned and his knees buckled. Keio Ohara was not finished with him yet. The tall Japanese held his opponent's wrist with one hand and used the other to lock the man's elbow in a straight-arm bar. Then he pivoted sharply, pulling the terrorist with him by the captive arm and abruptly drove the man face-first into a wall. The Irish thug slumped to the floor, leaving a trail of bloodstains on the wallpaper.

"That's Riley!" cried David. "He's headed for the stairs!"

Seamus Riley coughed, choking on the stink of cordite and the smoke of the grenades. All around him his men were dying. The cause was lost, but the battle was not over.

The Americans would pay!

New York City would pay!

22

GARY HEARD DAVID'S CRY and spun to see Riley fighting his way up the stairs.

The Canadian moved after him. Riley was his. He headed for the stairs with Ingram in hand.

Fire licked at the walls in the dining room, caught in the ruptured upholstery of the couch and an overstuffed chair. It poured new clouds of smoke into the room, choking billows of fog that burned the eyes and strangled the lungs.

The stairs were on fire. Riley leaped over the top riser as Gary plunged after him, beating at the flames that tried to consume his clothes. He saw Riley fall to the floor, and then the fire flared before him.

Gary broke through the flames, the fire frustrated by his wet clothing. He found the hall empty.

Riley, you son of a bitch, Gary thought, *where the hell are you?*

Ingram ready for action, Gary kicked in the first door and found a bathroom filled with smoke from the fire in the kitchen below. The floorboards were growing hot, beginning to smolder.

He backed into the hall, heard a noise and spun.

The noise came from a window frame, cracking under the heat of the fire that had caught in the walls. Gary moved to the next door.

It was a bedroom, which held army-surplus beds, set up for Riley's army. It was also empty.

Gary moved to the next room.

BELOW, THERE WERE A FEW SURVIVORS, the Atlanta "electrician" among them. He staggered from the house under Rafael's watchful eye and collapsed on the lawn, choking. His face was covered with soot and his hands were marked with third-degree burns; he was slipping into shock.

Yakov came up to him. "The bomb!" he said. "Where is the New York bomb?"

The electrician looked up, shook his head. "It's in the World Trade Center, but you fools are too late. It's blown."

"We cut the phone line!" said Rafael.

"It makes no difference. There's a backup, a radio switch. Seamus has the radio in his bedroom. It's too late."

The Phoenix Force agents whirled and looked at the house, which was a mass of flames.

"Gary's up there!" said Rafael.

"And so's Riley," said Yakov.

GARY KICKED IN ANOTHER DOOR and found another fiery bedroom. He started to turn back, then heard coughing. He moved into the room and saw Riley on his knees on the far side of the bed. The Irishman gasped for breath, trying to drag air into his tortured lungs; but the air was overheated, too hot for human life. Another minute and it would be too late for either of them.

"Riley!"

The Irishman looked at Gary and lunged toward the radio transmitter on a dresser. Gary held down the trigger.

Nothing happened. The Ingram misfired.

Choking with smoke, sobbing with frustration, the Irishman tried to reach the transmitter as Gary threw aside the Ingram.

The gutsy Canadian then dived headlong across the bed, grabbing Riley's head in midflight and smashing it into the corner of the dresser.

Manning quickly scraped himself off the floor, ready for any fight the man could muster. But Riley was stunned. He slowly rose, dazed and beaten. Blood poured from a large gash in his skull.

Smoke filled the room. Flames jumped menacingly. Manning knew the fight was now centered on survival: he had to get the hell out of the fireground.

Leaving the dazed Riley, he rushed to the door. The way was blocked with raging fire, ripping at the wood of the old house. He staggered back, hands up to protect his face from the burning horror. There was no way out through the inferno.

There was one way out of the building.

Manning grabbed Riley with two hands and placed the man in front of him. Riley put up little struggle, the life pulsing from his skull.

Using the terrorist as a shield, Manning rushed the second-floor window and crashed through. The fire roared after him; Riley screamed in front of him. The terrorist leader's face was riddled with shards of splintered glass.

Riley died the second he hit the ground, the weight and force of Manning pounding down on top of him. The Phoenix Force agent felt the life being crushed out of Riley, then his head struck soil and darkness reigned.

EPILOGUE

MACK BOLAN sat in the War Room at Stony Man Farm, relaxing, listening to Hal Brognola's account of how Bolan's Phoenix Force defused the Fury Bomb. Bolan wore a satisfied smile, and he listened with pride.

"Manning took the only route out of the fiery hell," Brognola said, excitement riding the waves of his voice as he wrapped up his report. "He grabbed Riley, used him as a shield and sailed through the window.

"Riley, the guys tell me, died instantly, his frame flattened like a goddamn pancake." Brognola emphasized the point by smacking his hands together in a violent clap.

Bolan watched as the big Fed sucked deeply on his stogie. Concern entered his voice.

"We're damn lucky, Hal, that Gary's okay."

"We sure are," Brognola agreed. "The doctors told me he'd be back on his feet in a week—and bitching long before then."

A strange silence enveloped the room as Bolan and Brognola let their thoughts roam; both men thought about Phoenix Force.

Phoenix Force, like Able Team, was an extension of Mack Bolan the man, and Mack Bolan the freedom fighter. Each time that extension was thrown into combat, Mack Bolan lived, breathed and battled with them in spirit. When victory was attained, Mack Bolan felt proud.

Bolan's and Brognola's thoughts broke at the same time. The two longtime friends looked at each other, knowing full well what the other had been thinking.

"Phoenix Force," Brognola said. "Five good men."

Bolan nodded, smiled and underlined the truism.

"Five *damn good* men."

PHOENIX FORCE

AN EXECUTIONER SERIES

#6 White Hell

MORE GREAT ACTION
COMING SOON!

America was being punished for imagined crimes. The Trans-Alaska pipeline, a jugular in the oil life-support system, had been hit by a vengeful enemy.

Phoenix Force flies to the ice-covered North in the dead of winter. If they fail to exterminate the fanatics fast, a foreign attack on a crippled U.S. will be inevitable.

Those who die in the encounter will be the lucky ones. The survivors face a white hell too hideous to imagine....

Watch for new Phoenix Force titles wherever paperbacks are sold.

Coming soon:

MACK BOLAN FIGHTS ALONGSIDE ABLE TEAM AND PHOENIX FORCE

in

STONY MAN DOCTRINE

A world in flames!

This thrilling mega-novel has changed in concept and development since our last announcement. To keep pace with events in today's world, Mack Bolan's greatest adventure has grown even bigger!

America stands alone against the most powerful military regime in history. In four days of horror, Mack Bolan and his Stony Man people are forced to exceed the authority of the President himself, just as Bolan has always fought above and beyond the law— because justice and survival are at stake!

''Understand this, all of you. This is the big one. This is 'dirty war.' No surrender!''

—*Mack Bolan*

Available soon wherever paperbacks are sold.

HE'S EXPLOSIVE.
HE'S UNSTOPPABLE.
HE'S MACK BOLAN!

He learned his deadly skills in Vietnam...then put them to use by destroying the Mafia in a blazing one-man war. Now **Mack Bolan** is back to battle new threats to freedom, the enemies of justice and democracy—and he's recruited some high-powered combat teams to help. **Able Team**—Bolan's famous Death Squad, now reborn to tackle urban savagery too vicious for regular law enforcement. And **Phoenix Force**—five extraordinary warriors handpicked by Bolan to fight the dirtiest of anti-terrorist wars around the world.

Fight alongside these three courageous forces for freedom in all-new, pulse-pounding action-adventure novels! Travel to the jungles of South America, the scorching sands of the Sahara and the desolate mountains of Turkey. And feel the pressure and excitement building page after page, with nonstop action that keeps you enthralled until the explosive conclusion! Yes, Mack Bolan and his combat teams are living large...and they'll fight against all odds to protect our way of life!

Now you can have all the new Executioner novels delivered right to your home!

You won't want to miss a single one of these exciting new action-adventures. And you don't have to! Just fill out and mail the coupon following and we'll enter your name in the Executioner home subscription plan. You'll then receive four brand-new action-packed books in the Executioner series every other month, delivered right to your home! You'll get two **Mack Bolan** novels, one **Able Team** and one **Phoenix Force**. No need to worry about sellouts at the bookstore...you'll receive the latest books by mail as soon as they come off the presses. That's four enthralling action novels every other month, featuring all three of the exciting series included in The Executioner library. Mail the card today to start your adventure.

FREE! Mack Bolan bumper sticker.

When we receive your card we'll send your four explosive Executioner novels and, absolutely FREE, a Mack Bolan "Live Large" bumper sticker! This large, colorful bumper sticker will look great on your car, your bulletin board, or anywhere else you want people to know that you like to "Live Large." And you are under no obligation to buy anything—because your first four books come on a 10-day free trial! If you're not thrilled with these four exciting books, just return them to us and you'll owe nothing. The bumper sticker is yours to keep, FREE!

Don't miss a single one of these thrilling novels...mail the card now, while you're thinking about it. And get the Mack Bolan bumper sticker FREE!

BOLAN FIGHTS AGAINST ALL ODDS TO DEFEND FREEDOM!

Mail this coupon today!

Gold Eagle Reader Service, a division of Worldwide Library
In U.S.A.: 2504 W. Southern Avenue, Tempe, Arizona 85282
In Canada: 649 Ontario Street, Stratford, Ontario N5A 6W2

FREE! MACK BOLAN BUMPER STICKER
when you join our home subscription plan.

YES. please send me my first four Executioner novels. and include my FREE
Mack Bolan bumper sticker as a gift. These first four books are mine to examine free for
10 days. If I am not entirely satisfied with these books. I will return them within 10 days
and owe nothing. If I decide to keep these novels. I will pay just $1.95 per book (total
$7.80). I will then receive the four new Executioner novels every other month as soon
as they come off the presses. and will be billed the same low price of $7.80 per ship-
ment. I understand that each shipment will contain two Mack Bolan novels. one Able
Team and one Phoenix Force. There are no shipping and handling or any other hidden
charges. I may cancel this arrangement at any time. and the bumper sticker is mine to
keep as a FREE gift. even if I do not buy any additional books.

NAME _____ (PLEASE PRINT)

ADDRESS _____ APT. NO.

CITY _____ STATE/PROV. _____ ZIP/POSTAL CODE

Signature _____ (If under 18. parent or guardian must sign.)

This offer limited to one order per household We reserve the right to exercise discretion in
granting membership If price changes are necessary. you will be notified
Offer expires August 31, 1983   166-BPM-PAB6